I0548213

QUILLS FROM AFRICA 30: LONG WALK TO HOME

Printed by Amazon Publishers Createspace

First Printing, 2017

ISBN: 978-1-989035-00-9 Paperback

ISBN: 978-1-989035-01-6 Electronic

Authors Without Boundaries Publishing
25 Auburn Meadows Avenue SE,
Unit 225,
T3M 2L3,
Canada.
www.authorswithoutboundaries.com

TABLE OF CONTENTS

Acknowledgements

It's been a great year; 2017. We have reached a peak and believe that our droplet of water has quenched the thirst of some while giving others some hope. The cfwriterz platform started out simply as a section of a personal blog. I wanted to do much more with my writing, the group had little more than twenty members to begin with. The stories shared were all my own stories but the vision was bigger than that; I wanted to have a home for writers other than myself.

We have grown in leaps and bounds. This year we have published the "Freedom Magazine" twice. This collection of our top stories is our way of giving the stage to African stories. We have run paid and unpaid writing challenges. This platform has become part of a real entity registered in Nigeria as CF Media and Brand PR Services.

The website (cfwriterz.com) is designed to give credit to writers, to promote self-publishing and promote a writing and reading culture among young Nigerians and also across Africa. This anthology in Collaboration with Authors Without Boundaries is our first international publication and which will be produced in print. We have connected with other business brands like the writeapp.co, viva-naija, designed.life, and many others. We have given our best.

With all this in mind, I appreciate the Ambassadors; volunteers who have helped to coordinate group events. I appreciate my family and friends who have supported in one way or another to see this writing community grow. Thank you and I hope you love this collection.

Oladeji Jonathan Damilola

Editor-In-Chief

Foreword

Quills from Africa 30: Long Walk to Home, was compiled by Oladeji Jonathan D. A collection of short stories and poems by aspiring authors some of whom have won awards for their literature works. It is a book of eclectic mix of short stories, some from real life stories and others from the fantasy world of the mind.

The setting of the stories exposes the reader to the land, the climate and the ways of African people. The authors are self-confident, creative and use imaginations that keep the reader captivated.

It is through these stories that they have created their sense of self and bring people together and expand their limited views of the world. It's encouraging to see young writers following their dreams.

Monica Kunzekweguta

Author/Publisher/ Speaker

Authors Without Boundaries

Sometime in April

by Oladeji Jonathan Damilola

I had briskly walked past a woman who seemed truly distressed enough to jump, it was April and the harmattan had stretched quite longer. I only turned because I suddenly realized she would jump. She stood dangerously close to the edge of Eko Bridge, it was early morning around the time. "Lagosians" were just coming away from the mosque. She had just enough time to take a plunge, before cars started to honk and traders peddle their wares past that spot. It's common to hear Nigerians boast about suicide being a white man's demon. Every few months there is someone who jumps from this bridge and every second there are a thousand more who contemplate jumping.

"Dupe, ahann Dupeee, Iwo ti e ni," she startled when she heard me call her name. I remembered her just as well as she remembered me. We had always been best of friends from way back in St. Dorothy high school. Only few of us had the privilege to call her native name back then, she was simply "Cleopatra" to most people. Ironically Queen Cleopatra whom she had admired so much killed herself by means of an asp bite on August 12, 30 BC.

Vicious and strong, Dupe was my first love when candy and milk sold for two pence apiece. Our children will never know there was such a time, when the kobo actually meant riches to my family and my father's allowance was one naira, fifty kobo.

She hurriedly fled the bridge on seeing me, she disappeared into the melee. The morning fog briefly settled on my face as I stood dazed at what I had just seen. Two weeks later I read of a woman who had jumped from Eko bridge, Dupe's name was all I saw as I hurried off the office premises. I found her home within the hour. The silence told of the distinct sense of loss, her mother sat in a cane chair, old and grey. The woman could not even cry, her face twitched intermittently but her sorrow was lost in her dying body.

I was about penning a condolence wish when I saw him, winking at a woman. You could see she had merely snatched a black scarf off some roadside stall, just to fit into the moody situation. her makeup jumped out from under her cowering brows. She smelt of airports, luggage and hotel baths, I got close enough to her while they whispered. She was uncomfortable but Dupe's husband was all over her, I noticed them maybe because I thought of how heartbroken I felt and expected him to be distraught.

"Don't you think you should have told me your wife died?"

"Tayo! and what difference…" he held her elbow quite a bit too long and whispered in her ears.

They hurried off to the Master's bedroom, I watched from the corner of my eye.

I waited till evening when most people had retired to their homes or taken to the kitchen courtesy of growling tummies. I remember when Dupe chose him over me, she said he made her float. I was just too fixated on pouring all my love on her, it was obsessive in her opinion. Kola was taller, he had a lot of girls crawling over him so she was spellbound at those little things he did.

"Kola let this wait, please let the Dead get some sleep" I listened closer, as zippers and buttons came undone. I was there at the door to the nursery Kola had built, where he had tortured Dupe with his dreams of babies. I heard the stories in snatches, he had haunted her existence all for her to birth something.

Now his hands were beneath another woman's skirt, while tears were still hot on countless faces. His right palm firmly held the curve of her left breast, his lips smacked lightly towing a line from the top of her head to her navel. He pulled off her dress and for a split second just stood and admired her naked body. His hands tugged at his erection as he closed the gap between them, she

8

moaned as he slid into her. He ravished her there in the same place where his now dead wife must have begged for him to love her. I felt nauseous and left the house planning all the different ways to commit murder I could think about. The bitterness I felt increased every time I had flashbacks of the images I saw at the house. I wept for Dupe. This was what she died for?

I waited a few months and saw that the new girl had received a nod from most of the family, they felt it was time to forget. It was barely six months and Kola had to move on, they hardly knew he had forgotten their daughter before she died. How could Dupe be so easy to fling aside? The only person I could share my pain with was Dupe's mother, she had suffered a stroke and could not reply when I visited.

"Mama, Dupe ti sun, but her sleep is not the kind she deserves," I looked into the eyes of the older woman, they had welled up with tears. I squeezed her hands and promised to do something, "...anything to make that man suffer for the miserable life Dupe lived with him." Dupe had sent me an email a few years back, she tried to sound casual but she could not hide that she was in an abusive union.

I texted Tayo late November; the new girl had no idea what I had planned. We met finally in January, I asked to take her on a date. Every day in the month, I sent her flowers and chocolate boxes, I distracted her eventually. Kola had started picking some signs from her attitude, he accused her of seeing someone and she told me. "You know I have his engagement ring," she twisted the engagement ring on her finger and smiled. We sat at a table somewhere in Ilupeju and just listened to Lagos buzzing all around us. I smiled back at her.

"Do you love me?" she said,

I thought about my answer for a bit.

"What would you say if I asked you to return to London?"

"What? No! I think this is a mistake. I need to leave"

9

She made to get up but I restrained her. Clearly, she deserved what was coming to her.

"I don't love you Tayo, you are just as evil as Kola."

Her smile slowly faded as she held my gaze. "What did you just say?"

"Look at you Tayo, established and doing fine on your own, you had to get yourself into another man's mess. Why didn't you leave when you knew he had just lost his wife?"

Her eyes started to droop, the morphine in her wine was starting to kick in. I had spiked the drink before she could notice. I pulled her up from the chair and strapped her arm around my neck. We staggered to the car while I signaled those watching that she was drunk.

"You will soon start to experience nausea, delusions, and some confusion. Your muscles would fail, coma sets in and then you die." I drove towards the beach as I spoke, I sent Kola a text from her phone asking to meet at the beach.

Hello honey,

I will be there in a few, get me keep my wine chilled as usual.

His reply came in just as I finished setting her down, at their usual place. I had watched them for long enough and like every human their routine was what made my work so easy. They had a secret spot and I could see him approaching it, her feet were in the water and she looked like she was just taking a nap. He tiptoed as he got closer, he must have been thinking to surprise her. I jumped him from behind knocking the wind out of him. That gave me enough time to strangle him with the rope I had brought for that purpose. He struggled to grab my arm, his legs violently trashed as he tried to break loose from my grip.

Tayo's lifeless body got swept off the beach and then he realized she was dead, he seemed to lose all his strength and just started to plead as he choked in my hands.

I realized quite too late that he was paying way more than the sin he had committed. He may have drove Dupe to her death but he was better than the monster I had become. She had a choice but I was giving him none. Tears streamed down my face as his body went limp. I had not only lost Dupe to this man, I had also lost my sanity to him.

The Writer

Jonathan writes stories about faith, politics and sexuality. He started and leads the cfwriterz.com group and platform because he believes every story deserves to be told. His blog; jonathanoladeji.com started out as a place to find escape and open up without restraint, now he teaches skills that help writers to benefit from self-publishing. He talks about content marketing ideas for small businesses. He recently started his Masters Degree in Real Estate at the University of Pretoria, South Africa. His stories and articles have been shared and published on reputable African and international websites and journals.

Mobile: +27635280244

Email: jonathanoladeji@gmail.com

Facebook: Damilola Jonathan Oladeji

Instagram: damilolajonathan

Twitter: @De_Furst

11

12 AM

by Oluwatosin Joel

12:00AM

"That is the house" I pointed from a distance dropping my hand in a flash to avoid being seen

"It's going to be a very difficult mission to carry out considering the security placement and most especially that her surly weird looking dog," Akpan said

"So, in other words, it's a mission impossible?" I asked in a despondent voice looking him straight in the eyes.

"Yea it's looking so but Nothing is Impossible, even the movie Mission Impossible turned out to be possible" He responded with a faint smile

This response from him lit my joy from within me, feeding my face a flush of a smile. I knew that if there was anyone that could handle this task, it would be Akpan. I admire his strength. I wonder most times how one could be so full of perfection and with almost no flaws. He was my description of Samson—the guy who killed a Lion in the bible. I knew that with Akpan on this mission I was in safe hands. Though this was my first perilous mission, I did not feel so antsy. I was all calm and collected. I mean, Akpan was involved, so why should I?

So what time are we going on this mission?" I asked

"Tonight.12 AM" He replied with all determination

"12 am?"

"Do you have any problem with that?" He gave me this spine-chilling looks

"I have all problems with that dude! That's too late!" The inner me said that though only I could hear it.

"I am all cool with it" I responded, looking like all was well.

***

11:58AM

I was at our meeting spot. I had created another me with blankets and pillow on my bed to deceive my mum into believing that I was in. I had told her earlier in the day that I don't want to be disturbed and she should not bother coming to check me up which is so typical of her. "Does she not sleep?" I ask myself this most times.

Every night she parades the house with insecticides, going from room to room on a mission to clamp down on every flying creature; an unending battle that is almost always lost. This act of hers calls me back to reality from dreamland. The cacophony of sounds she produces during her engagement with mosquitoes is a nightmare. "

Mummy!!! Not again! You are disturbing me" I keep saying these words when the "Her VS mosquitos" battle is on. She just looks at me coldly and continues with her war on the poor flying creatures who are just trying to survive by feeding on blood.

I had fixed my lock on my door, which had been spoilt since devil knows when. Well, I just had to because I was so sure mum would still pay a visit to my room tonight, despite my warning. She promised not to, but I don't need a detective to tell me she was lying. She was going to peep from my door lock, which was why I cloned myself on the bed with pillows and blanket.

It was 12 AM and Akpan wasn't here yet. I stood at the back of a Neem tree. I needed it to serve as a cover for me while I studied the environment. I could not express my feelings. I have never been out this late.

"I am not scared," I said, albeit in a voice breaking from cold fear.

The weather was starting to act along. The wind played spooky familiar sounds to my ears. It sounds like the same wind that blew when Kelan was out in the woods being chased by vampires in Blood Diaries, my latest seen movie.

13

"I am not scared" I reiterated the words again. They were my only company in this frightful neighbourhood.

I pulled out the dark gloves I kept in my pocket and put them on. I was starting to feel frigid and sultry at the same time. I rubbed my two palms together in a very fast motion. I have always wondered why they do that in movies but I just got to understand that, involuntarily, it produced a sort of warmth and calmness. I looked around; still, Akpan was nowhere to be found. I clicked on my led wrist watch. It was 12:08 AM. I felt comfortless

"Akpan where are you?"

I couldn't go back home this time. The security gate definitely must have been locked, plus it's so risky. I had it planned out that after tonight's mission; I would be spending the night over at Akpan's place, leaving after the first cock crows. But now, it's looking impossible.

This mission was looking not possible. I was giving in to fear. To make matters worse, as I looked up the tree that served as my buckler, I saw glowing eyes. Not one or two, but they were all over the tree. At this sight, I took to my heels. I just kept racing.

When I believed I had run enough to escape the piercing eyes, the tree stood, I took a halt. I could hear my heartbeat. I sat on a pavement to regain my strength. I wasn't finding things funny. After minutes of rest, I decided to spend the night on the pavement I sat on. It had a rectangularly shaped figure like my bed but the difference was that it felt hard while my bed was soft.

Well, it had to be hard since it was made from brick. I checked my time in bid to set a waking alarm, the time said 12:40 AM, I set my alarm to 4 AM. That was the time my estate security gate would be opened.

It was a full moon night. I lay down on this pavement I hired to be my bed for the night. I couldn't close my eyes. My ears would not stop hearing strange sounds or could it be my imagination? I couldn't tell. All I knew was that sounds were echoing; scary ones at that.

14

The moon was becoming brighter and was coming closer to where I laid. The light the bright moon produced lit the spot I slept on so that I could see everything around me, even the most infinitesimal object. I opened my eyes wide as I saw another pavement that looked similar to the one I laid on, but this was full of dried flowers.

I opened my eyes wide when I read out loud, unconsciously "MRS MARGRET OLOLADE LAID TO REST ON 5TH MARCH, 2005" I instantly sat up. Facing me was a boldly written epitaph which read "CHIEF OKAFOR IKEMEFUNA BURIED ON 3RD OF JUNE, 2009". I sprung up from where I sat. I was in a cemetery; I had been lying on someone's grave. Chilly sensations ran down my spine. I felt dead but alive.

Cemeteries had always been my greatest fear. I remembered during my granny's funeral, I was unable to follow them to where she was buried. I stayed outside because I believed that the corpses were going to rise and kill me, just like I had always seen in horror movies.

Now, not only was I in a cemetery, I also laid on someone's grave!

"Oh no! Oh no! I didn't just lay there"

"Yes, you did and who are you?" said a strange voice

I was the only one there and still, I heard a voice

"Who talked!? Who is there!?" I exclaimed with the last courage I could muster. I wasn't seeing anyone. I balled my head around with all fake readiness and with my fists out to wrestle anyone that popped out from the night.

"I am CHIEF OKAFOR IKEMEFUNA," The strange voice said, in tow with a cold laugh

The name sounded familiar to me. My head tried processing where I had heard the name.

"CHIEF OKAFOR IKEM............"

Before I could spell out the name, I remembered it was his tomb I laid on. I knew I should not be here. I took to my heels. I

15

couldn't feel my feet touching the ground as I ran. After another long run, I halted. Again. I stayed at the side of an abandoned bus. I rested my back on it, gathering air. Not too long, a bright torchlight was pointed directly at my face. The brightness of this torch showed that the person behind it must have powered it from a transformer.

"Who is there!?" The voice exclaimed

Before I could give any response, I had been grabbed by my belt.

***

I sat in the back seat of mum's car as she drove home slowly. My head was faced downward with disappointment. Mum had come to bail me from the police station. Akpan's uncle had also come to bail him out as well. What I didn't know was that Akpan later showed up at our meeting point 10minutes after the agreed time. So, since he didn't see me, he decided to carry out the mission alone, leading to his eventual arrest and being taken to the police station. We both landed in the same station. We narrated our story to the policemen.

"So, you went through all this because you wanted to get your ball that was kicked into the compound?" A fat dark bald policeman asked

We nodded with both our faces down.

"Why didn't you go knock on the gate and explain to them that your ball was mistakenly kicked into their compound?"

I and Akpan looked at ourselves for a sec

"We never thought of that option"

This lit up a laugh at the police station. It just dawned on us that we were practically fools.

Mum had said nothing so far. Her silence always meant death to me. The car was so silent. Even Tomiwa my 2years old junior brother that sat next to me didn't make his usual noise and cries. He just fixated his big round balled eyes on me (His eyes remind me of Aderinto Victoria glasses, she was the shortest girl in class.

16

Did I just say in class, I meant in the whole school? Though some say she is the shortest girl in the world) that's by the way, he stared at me as he sucked his pinky finger. I looked back at him. I could read his mind. He called me a fool. The inner me replied him that I wasn't a fool and it wasn't my fault that I had to carry out such a foolish mission. It was a conversation of the mind.

It was a long drive home, not because our home was far from the police station nor because of all what had just happened, it was because mum was still a learner in driving.

The Writer

Taiwo Oluwatosin Joel goes by the pen name Theo-ziny Joel. He was born on 24th of July, 1994 in Lagos, Nigeria. He is a Nigerian born writer/poet/script writer. He is known for his tragic, yet humorous African contemporary style of writing. His short fiction stories have been published on various websites also on radio. Few of his works can be found on his blog zinysdiary.wordpress.com a fast-growing online blog. He is currently working on his debut book publication- A collection of short fiction stories, and lives in Ogun, Nigeria.

Mobile: +2348124735845

Email: theozinyjoel@yahoo.com

Facebook: Theo-ziny Joel

Instagram: Theo_ziny

Whatsapp: +2348124735845

Affected

by Chioma Blessing Onyechi

In this country, it is always very difficult for a single parent to take proper care of their children, especially when it's a woman. My dad is late and I'm the third amongst three of his offspring. When dad was alive things went well. We had laughter at home and I had ample time to play with him. I'm what you might want to call 'daddy's girl'. My father had a very good friend, Uncle Charles. He has a wife but she's rarely ever available because of her kind of work. Uncle Charles always takes special care of me. He isn't just a friend, over the years he has become family.

I love him a lot, he has been of great help to us after our father's passing. Being a single mother isn't easy. My mother takes up two jobs so she can meet the demands of her family. Uncle Charles and his wife are her auxiliaries. But then he still reserves a soft spot for me, always at my beck and call. I like to think it is because I'm the youngest of the three children and maybe because everyone is worrying that the sportive side of me had died with dad. I no longer spare time to even play with the neighborhood kids. I had folded into myself with the briskness of a millipede. I'm always home alone in the evenings; while mum is still at work, my eldest brother and my other sibling would go where ever the rambling takes them.

I often wonder why Uncle Charles always dots on me. He always uses the line, "your father was my friend and I promised him I'm going to look after you" and "you know we have a special bond" I don't quite understand what this bond was. Not until the night I turned fifteen. Because his wife was away indefinitely, he had asked my mum that I come over to his house to keep his visiting niece company. I'm sunk in the sofa fixating on the giant plasma TV when he perched beside me on the sofa.

"good evening uncle" I stutter, trying to widen the gap between us.

"I bought you some birthday gifts" he said shifting to close the gap between.

He placed his hands on my thigh "you know we have a special bond and I gave your father my word that I would take care of you"

His hand on my thigh felt as strange as people giggling at a funeral. I shoot him a stare but he held his gaze. After that night, I begin to feel jumpy and uncomfortable around him. He noticed it and moved to placate me. He said it was normal to feel the way I'm feeling. Then it graduated to everyday groping and tickling. After an intense groping the following morning, he laid on top of me, there was an intense pain between my legs, I could barely breathe. Afterwards he keeps saying,

'Don't tell anyone it's only fun.' Then he cuddled me and said, 'We're friends now,'

I didn't understand what had happened. I knew it was wrong, but I couldn't tell anyone. I got home after that night and I resorted to staying indoors, I didn't talk to anyone, and I never let my mother or brother come close. Weeks later, he came to visit us, all the while he talked with my mom, he kept staring at me, I knew the look, it was the same look he gave me that night, I got uncomfortable so I went to my room, "She's been acting strange lately" I heard my brother say.

I laid on my bed, hoping that I'm only having a terribly nightmare and that it will all go away. When silence replaced the voices outside, I suppose he is gone. My door slowly opened, I didn't turn because I suspected it was John my immediate older brother coming to throw his usual banter, but no, it was uncle Charles.

"Good girl.." he whispers into my ear, I quaked in fear. A flashing image of what he did to me cropped up in the mirror of my mind, I sprang up to my feet to find him smiling, I couldn't bear to look at him anymore.

"I know you liked it, with time it would only get better" he started to touch me, but I pushed his hands away. "Your mother has gone to get some stuff, Ben has gone to the field and I sent John on an errand "O my God! He smiled wickedly "I sent John on an errand" tears trickle down my face "This would be quick and you'll love it" he says pulling me to himself.

It became more regular and I felt helpless to tell anybody about what was happening. I wanted to make it stop but I was afraid to speak out, because a part of me didn't want to get him into trouble. My mum thinks highly of him and he helps our family unflinchingly. I couldn't concentrate in school, I also had problems remembering things, I transfer aggression in school because it was the only place I could express the burning anger inside me. Once I got suspended from school because I had used my pencil to stab a boy who had tried to touch my breast, I tried to explain to the principal what he was trying to do, but the boy insisted he was only trying to take off the bug he saw on my sweater, my mother was called to pick me up, she still didn't believe what I said, and she hit me hard that day. It only made my rebellion worst.

After my suspension, I stopped doing any of my school works. My mom was too busy with work to notice my change in attitude. He also told me to wear skirts, I told my tell mum to buy me jeans to protect myself, but I couldn't explain why I needed them, so I never got any. I didn't know how to make it stop. Months later we had sex education, and then I felt I could summon the courage to talk to my mom.

One day, my mom and I are in the kitchen "Mum, when is it good for a girl to have sex?" she gave me a once-over in disbelieve glance.

"The best suitable time is when a girl is married"

"What would you do if someone you know takes advantage of a little girl" she was taken aback by that question

"Jennifer! Where are you getting all of these ideas from?"

"What if I tell you Uncle Charles touches me where he isn't supposed to?"

"Shut up!!!..."

"I'm telling you mum" I tried to explain to her, but she couldn't believe anything I say

That day, I got a serious beating. Mother warned me never to speak of it again, on the grounds that I was an ungrateful child.

"After all he did for us, you still have the guts to assume that about him?" she'd said angrily

Now, my only hope of making him pay was shattered, I realized I have no one to run to, what is it with all grownups, and why are they finding it hard to believe me? I knew I had to fight and stand up for myself.

Weeks later, he came again, my mom had gone to drop off a document at a neighbour's house, I knew she'd back soon. The house is silent. I froze at the sight of him,

"What are you doing here?" I ask trying my best to act normal. "My mother isn't home and my brothers are out" I hoped he picks the hint, because I was certain mum will be home soon. He looked lustfully at me and started coming towards me. I wore the image of a frightened girl so he wouldn't notice the change in my attitude.

"Naughty girl" He whispered already panting like a dog on heat. "I've missed you" he said as soon as his placed his hands on my breast, I jerk in pain as he squeezed. "where are you mum, come on?!" I cry in my mind.

"Please...please" I plead.

"I like it when you beg, naughty girl"

"Please I beg you...please not today. I feel sick"

"That's because you missed me, come let me fill you" he said huskily, I knelt down holding this leg, my mom should be back by now, I was beginning to regret my plan, and hoped to God she wasn't held up.

"I beg you in God's name uncle, don't do this please"

"It'll only be a minute" he whispers into my ears as he dragged me up, he pinned me to the sofa and tries to force himself into me.

"You bastard!" my mother roared as she barged into the sitting room, just as I was about to give up "get yourself off my child"

She launched herself at him, throwing all manner of stuff at him, anything she laid her hands on.

"You're a monster!" my mother kept raining abuses on him. Soon the house was clustered with neighbors.

"You fool!!" he snapped "You never had time for her! I give her all the attention she needs, I pay her fees and feed you and your kids. What do you think I am? Santa Clause?"

That statement enraged my mom further. She ran straight to the kitchen and returned charging towards him with a knife. He made for the door as neighbours began to scream, some dazed and some trying to stop my mother. He ran out leaving his trousers behind. The crowd trails behind, hot on his heel, as my mother ran out after him. He impulsively tries to traverse the road but an oncoming truck ran him over. We all came to stand over his body.

Now I'm 22, I still picture his motionless body and I have no regrets that he died. One less scum bag.

The Writer

Chioma Blessing Onyechi hails from Anambra state, Nigerian. She lives in Bauchi state and is currently an undergraduate of computer science department in the Federal Polytechnic Bauchi state. And also awaiting admission in the Abubakar Tarawa Balewa University Bauchi, where she enrolled for a Direct Entry to study Information Technology. She has a passion for writing and has written a handful of fictional novels.

Mobile: +2348166675961

Email: ocblessing.dc@fptb.edu.ng

Facebook: Chioma B Onyechi

1814

by Olamide Adio Olanrewaju

1814.

"Love your curves and all your edges. All your perfect imperfections."

You are dancing with her. Your wife, lover, in the most absurd setting. And this is not the first time, but it certainly will be the last. At least for this life of hers.

"You're my end and my beginning. Even when I lose I'm winning"

The hospital room is colder than you remember. You've been here before. 1912? 1979? 1994? Time has stolen your memory. She is crying, her stepping is tremulous, her shaved head is rested on your shoulder. She sniffs. She sobs. She sobs. She breaks.

"How many times do I have to tell you? Even when you're crying you're beautiful too."

Touché, John legend. You think.

"It is not fair my prince." She says It is not fair.

"This moment is perfect." You whisper; I'll be waiting. Come back to take me and lead me far away.

She nods. Sobs. Sniffs. She looks up at you with her cat eyes, sucking you into her world. Then she convulses. She is shaking violently like turbulent waves. Blood is seeping out of her gritted teeth. She has bitten her tongue.

"Nurse! Nurse!!" Your screams border hysterics.

There is something about death and humanity that has intrigued you through time —an equally interesting phenomenon. We always fight. Even when we know it is inevitable. And death never resists our futile battles with it. It knows it will win, it needs only be patient. But what happens when we live to die and then live to die again? Do we win that way? Does immortality cure this bane?

The nurses surge in like bees to Queen Bee, all armed to the teeth with injections, defibrillator, a doctor, and about anything to resuscitate your hope. But you and your lover know it's all a facade. Your beloved will die.

You are weeping, because it doesn't matter how many times you live this place, this moment, this transition still never gets better. Loss and time are accursed accomplices. One alleviates the other and the other accentuates one; a brutal cycle. This is not the first time she will die. You both know it will not be the last. The doctor holds two fingers to her neck, searching for a nonexistent pulse. You still look to him nonetheless, play the part of a hopeful partner. He raises his head, shakes his head. Finality.

Goddess.

The birds that scoop your waters cry with their feathers like raining ethers.

The fishes that swim your body tweet their grief in hyper-sibilant hisses.

The death that touches your gaze breathes. Hear my plead. Bleed my

lover to me. Death, give me back my loss. For the gods lied

about their curse, its cause shouldn't curse this cause.

***

1814

It was here your love story began —in the lush settlement ensconced in a fertile jungle. Naive and harmless. You were teenagers inexperienced in the art of love. Taken only by its beauty, for when love is rationalized, its beauty dies, and it is only adolescence that could love so recklessly. Your father was king,

26

and she, a commoner. The perfect premise for a troubled love story. She was a virgin priestess, sewn to the hips of a river goddess. But love demands more than we have, it pushes, it forges, it perseveres: and so, did your love. Your love was forbidden —and that in itself is sacred, it is the forbidden fruit every man wants to eat. You would lie together on a rainy day, in the shrine of this goddess, holding on to the affection you shared, and hope, hope that the goddess would see the fire in this love and leave you be. The day she gave you what she pledged to the goddess in the absence of the chief priest, you had both burned the embers of love. As you touched, the shrine burnt, before your eyes stood the river goddess herself, lightening in her eyes, angry and betrayed. You and your lover had stood naked before her as she cursed. You begged. She cursed. You irked.

"Our love will never die!" You'd screamed, holding her protectively, daring the goddess with your stare.

"So be it," the goddess replied, "it will be your blessing and your curse." Then she vanished in a whiff of celestial white and aqua.

The chief priest would subsequently burst in to catch you both naked.

This was the first time you'd both die. It has been a long time, but you still remember the fear her eyes held—and yours mirrored—as you were both dragged through the village by circumcised horses. The taste of stones hurled at you by the villagers — even your father. The smell of burning flesh. The sight of sand. So much sand. She was buried alive while you watched; screaming, burning at the stake for your crime of unbridled love against the river goddess.

The curse of the goddess was for you both to get lost in love. Again, and again, you'd both meet through time, fall in love, only for one to die and leave the other distraught. Then the search would begin until the survivor found the lost one again, to die or to lose—whichever the case may be. You always prefer to be the one to die, because living without her is torture, and your existence tethers at the periphery of the knowledge that she is out

27

there for you to find. But you hate the thought of her feeling this way, being in this place, so you share the burden.

Goddess,

The earth won't forgive us.

When it does, like a stubborn bone, it spits me back to her, another beginning.

The winds won't carry us home.

Like the lightening of the Thunder God, it tatters us both; whole.

Death, give my lover back to me.

Strain your ears and hear my plead.

***

1967

It was you who died prior to this time. Plunged in the middle of a war between countrymen; you would find that death, love, religion, immortality, and war all have uncanny similarities. You had always felt something amiss until you were forced to fight the Biafrans.

You would find her as a prostitute, raped to near death by your fellow soldiers. And they would urge you to go around on her too. Bolstered by their shouts, by cigarettes, alcohol, and the morality of war, you'd climb her, and as you became one, the memories of your shared past lives flooded you. You would shoot her there yourself, for that body had been tainted. You would wander; searching for decades, not ageing—for once one found the other, ageing ceases abruptly.

It would be forty-three lonely years before you found her again in the arms of another man in the University of Ibadan. Every time, she had taken the same body, the same face, the same beauty. Your memories of love here would be shambolic. Her, teaching you how to twerk. You, teaching her to belch louder in the school library. Her, teaching you French. You, writing unfinished cantos in her honour.

Love is not love, love that forgets. You'd find solace in your meshed past lives. And regardless of how short the stay, of how many times you were separated —scattered like seeds on a farm through time, marked by the pain of replayed history like a slave, weaker, but whole—, you'd always return to each other. Burning stronger, fiercer than your love hitherto had. You find respite in that one fact.

Goddess,

The fires of your curse wane, your spell dispels.

My lover has died, here are my tears.

Flown to the ethers again as stars to court the earth.

Drink from her skull, but be sure to return her before fall.

I wander again, a man without land.

Love is the seed these tears plant.

And you've made a bad thing immortal.

***

TODAY

A teardrop falls with each step you take. You're falling farther behind the stretcher driving her to the morgue.

"Take heart, sir. The Lord giveth and he takes." The decrepit doctor says. "You believe in God sir? One day, we will all rise not to die again."

Religion is an elaborate illusion. It removes us from our being and connects us to something larger than us —a God. This connection pales death, balms the pain of love. What happens when you are bigger than religion? How does your pain dissipate?

You think of stars, predestination, and the invisible thread that binds your soul and that woman being wheeled away. You had both planned to get married —something you'd never done in your past lives— before she got diagnosed with lung cancer. Slowly she withered away again from your grasp. And you'd held her today, crying on her corpse, oblivious of the next time you'd find her. Ten? Twenty? Thirty? Forty? Fifty years?

Time of death. 1814 hrs. The doctor finishes.

In the cold hospital room some feet behind you, John Legend reaches the denouement.

"Coz all of me loves all of you."

The Writer

Olamide is a student of Theatre arts at the premier university of Ibadan. He is a multi award winning writer, artist, and an outlandish lover of cats. He believes the love of dodo is the beginning of wisdom. He also likes the smell of old books.

Mobile: +234 **8181271208**

Email: Fortheloveofdodo@yahoo.com

Facebook: Olamide Olanrewaju

Instagram: the.anonymousartist

About A Broken Family

by Adewusi David

ABOUT A BROKEN FAMILY

The white walls. The flowing white ceilings. The endless sound of footsteps. The women in white and their silent chatters with the patients who still had the boldness to smile and gist. The afternoon visits of the flies. The slow movement of the clock, steadily and silently ticking out your life. The tip-tap-tip sound of the very rare rains on the window panes.

That period of time when your own life flashes before your own eyes, like a black and white movie; that period, you notice the littlest of things. During this time, your whole life becomes bright headlights deep in the dark, gradually becoming dim and finally vanishes. This time, the big things break into tiny bits of worries, incessantly tickling the raunchiest part of your bowels.

The nurses are the worst hypocrites. They know what you are going through but will still go ahead and ask, "How are you feeling ma?"

You would be torn between two choices- to say how exactly you felt, emotional and physically. Or just lie and save your strength. Or maybe the nurses mean how you feel physically? They know you never feel well. Maybe it is just duty to ask. Your weak lips break into a smile, "Nurse Kike, I'm fine."

A thermometer is fixed in your mouth. They want to know how hot or cold you have become. Hot means the pills administered will be double. Cold means worse. It is an imminent sign, especially in the feet.

***

Time used to be the weapon of the brave. Its rhythmic movement sends signals to your brains, waves to your ears, odour to your nostrils. And then it remains a day or two to spend with the life machine. The machine with its 'beeping' voice telling you the

31

stories of lives he had almost saved. It was a life machine, but we needed a life to learn how to live... And love.

Your life plays slowly before your own eyes. In the nurses, you see your young self. You remember the first time with him. He was the patient in room 004; he had malaria. An injection had created a love story. One which even family and children couldn't tear apart.

Then came the kids. They were three in number, minus the dead one. The one who wants to marry, the optimistic one and the youngest one. You remember the times you weren't there. The times their words echoed plead and attention in your ears. The many times you pushed them to the maid to have their assignments done. Those times you had those confrontations with the teenage girls. They are no longer kids, they are now females on the brink of adulthood.

You want to wish. But no, you tell yourself. Your life is a done deal, and such deals require no backing out. In life, you have learned that certain people have to be the one who leaves. Inevitably you ask yourself why you are not the kind of person who stays. Maybe you aren't worth staying. Maybe people like you are meant to be laid in the ground so the foundations of Earth will remain in position. Maybe... Maybe... Maybe...

Then again, your problems become compounded.

Your children walk in with blank faces. You are a mother, you should see through the blank stares. Yes, you see. You see the hidden tears, the fake laughs, the hidden meaning of the long stares. You break the silence.

-Are you all planning something? A surprise?

Silence. Every one of them smiles; a shrewd one.

-Is someone ready to say something?

The eldest one begins; her marriage is a few weeks away.

-We talked to the family.

-Y'all thought that'll surprise me? Your biggest wish.

A small, forced smile creeps on your face. You know where the conversation leads, but you are too scared to take the path. You don't want to leave your children heartbroken. But they all possess broken hearts already, coupled with a broken home. A home gripped by the fearsome hands of mortality.

-The doctor says...

-Mother no.. No doctor mom. We changed the wedding date.

You are slightly irritated. It is one you can't avoid. You strain your ears to continue listening.

-They want you there. We do.

-But I don't want me there. I am going to a place far away from here. Leaving you guys is enough!

The youngest of the girls speak up. Her voice sends waves through your body. A kind of wave that makes you feel guilty. One which invigorates your body and reminds you that in a few days, you'd be totally unable to feel anything, including this feeling.

-Mommy, are you scared by death?

Nothing surprises you anymore, a symptom of dying.

-I'm not scared by death. It's dying that scared me.

-Scared?

-Yes, scared. At this point, I try to just appreciate what I have left. But in those last final seconds, when my life stares at me like an assassin. I know I will be afraid. Not afraid by dying itself, but of its meaning.

-What does it mean?

-Hmm. It means you will be without me. Without a tall woman as a mother. Daddy will come home and no one would be there to kiss him on his cheeks. He will call the maid and one of you will have to take his bag to his bedroom.

-Mommy, don't talk like...

-Then the whole scene will reek of my absence...

-Stop it, ma.

It is the second daughter. The only one that remains herself in spite of the danger. She is a made euphemism. Her long hair and dark eyes hide the fear and anxiety she feels. But her face shows up bright and bold. You believe she's the strongest. But she isn't. A strong human that can't let his feelings go, like a stray bird, is he really a strong human? Or what's strength? Is it our ability to hide behind a façade of pain and come out looking bold? Or break through the wall of fear and pain while letting the hot, sticky pot of anger, fear, anxiety, sadness gnaws at your heart? You might never know; your time is short.

Then the father walks in. Your husband. You remember his face. He looks like he looked years before you married-- thin, tall with a burning excitement in his eyes; they never seem to leave.

-Are you okay, honey?

 -I am. I'm leaving soon.

-To where?

-To wherever this road leads.

-What are you saying?

You keep silent. Your mouth burns with words but the false excitement in it hold your withered tongue. You call her name. You believe it's the last time you ever will. So, you call it again.

-Anita, go ahead with the wedding on the proposed date.

-No, mummy. We all want you to be there.

-I will go with the memory of not coming to your wedding. That's less heartbreaking. What is more heartbreaking is leaving you to him and not come visiting after nine months to bathe the new man in the house? What's more heartbreaking is for me to stare down at you when the heavy turmoil of marriage falls on you. I will stare at you helplessly. Today. I want no tears...please.

34

But the tears wouldn't stay in your eyes either. Like Flash runs down a Skyscraper, they run down your cheeks with enviable speed. You take a look at all of them. Husband and kids. You continue.

-Anna...

Her gentle euphemistic hands rest on yours. You force a smile.

-Have you seen a potter at work?

-Yes, mom. Mom where's this...

-Like that clay, have you ever seen your life that way?

Silence.

-Our lives are clays. We often get it wrong. We don't always need to mould it into what we want. At times we are made what we want by nature. It only takes time to realize we've been moulded. A useless clay will form a hard path in the hot days, endlessly transporting people to their destinations. But on a rainy day, Anna.

Silence. A louder one.

-It throws people off it. It becomes slippery. Then, only wise and folks with common sense can cross the path.

-Mom...

Her touch on your hand has become a fearsome grip.

-It's better to stay unmolded than to be moulded by someone. Then a bridge becomes a cup.

The little girl speaks, obviously, your new-found knowledge amazes her.

-Does it mean I can't design my life?

-No... You can, always. But my baby, with your hands and with your heart.

Silence. They all slowly rush to you. A beep goes off in one of those machines you can't remember its name. Your breathing's changed. A man in white walks in and puts a mask over your face; an oxygen mask. Something with a sharp edge pierces your skin, causing an unmerited relief. Your eyes close...

***

Your large eyes open to faces staring blankly into yours. You are startled, but too weak to even react.

-Mom...

-It's today ma. We thought you were gone. Mom...

You try to speak but your whole body tells you not to. It's the wedding.

And it's the day you leave. It's the day you cross the lever.

***

Everyone in the ward is doing something. Including you; you are screaming. A child is stuck in your vagina. The pain is unexplainable. He is there. His hands are glued to yours. You keep your eyes on him for strength- emotional and physical.

-He's a boy!

You no longer feel the head in your legs. But your vagina hurts badly. He no longer holds you, his hands are busy with the red baby but his eyes are still on you; promising, silently telling you he loves you.

But the baby dies three months later.

That is how you sink into your pit of depression. You have three girls, but where's the boy to immortalize the family's name?

***

-Do you love him?

-Of course, mom, I do...

-Are you sure?

Tears have welled up in the eyes of everyone present.

-Yes mum...

36

-Protect it my baby... Fight for your love. What we do for love is fight. But in a war, you should always know when to surrender...

-I love you mom... But I can't fight... I can't even think.

-Yes, I know. Me too. It is time to surrender...

-No... No! No! Mum. No...

She places her head on your laps and you run your hand through her hair. You feel her warm tears on your laps and your heart finds it hard to beat.

-White is a sacred color. Don't stain the pretty gown with your tears.

The little one speaks, amidst her tears.

-I will miss you mom. When will you come to get me?

-You will join me when the time is right... But when you need me, look deep into the sky, appreciate the stars, drown yourself in the beauty of the moon. And I will be right there in your heart, whispering old tales of Moses and the Israelites.

-Mum I love you.

-I love you more than you can imagine baby.

It is at this moment the man places his hand on your forehead. The kids sit on your bed. They all hug you.

Then you remember everything. Your first kiss. First sex with him. Your eldest daughter's first birthday. Your affair with one of your patients and his forgiveness. His love. The kids' complaints.

Then you close your eyes because the emotions can almost tear open your heart. You, for the last time let the tears fall down your cheeks. You don't care anymore. You have lived a life you designed with your own hands.

***

And it's the next morning.

The Writer

David is a young writer whose principles borders on love, which remains the reason for our existence. He lives in a house on a hill, overlooking a street of struggling dreams.

Mobile: +2348069027002

Email: Blazedupdave@gmail.com

Facebook: David G. David

Adanne

by Eguzoro Sylvia Chijioke

She knows hopelessness.

She walks into the compound slowly, shoulders slouched. She looks around slowly, then frantically. She throws her handbag anywhere and dashes to a corner. Grunts, moans, hand gripping her stomach, hand on the wall. She walks back to pick her bag and swipes at the tears on her face. She goes to stand in front of their room.

"Aunty welcome." Urenna says to her.

"See the marks all over my body," she says, already taking off her blouse. "They are love bites. That's the name they call it. I went to see him again. He calls them his stamp. I won't be able to wear some of my clothes for now." She shrugs down the blouse.

They are all over her upper body; but more on the skin of her upper breasts. Fair skinned, she loves a little of her cleavage in view. Maybe that attracted him.

"He loves me." She continues.

She sighs.

"I know he loves me."

She sighs again.

"He should love me." She says in a small voice, head bowed, lip in-between her teeth.

She walks up to where I am seated – on a wooden stool in front of the only window of our room- washing the plates.

"There is food in the house? I should eat. I never eat at his house. I pretend to not be hungry when he offers. I am hungry though, but I need my transport money complete."

"Okay." Urenna replies.

39

"Ure," she says, facing her and clasping both hands immediately. "I'm not stupid. Believe me. You believe me, yes?"

"Adanne—"

A hand to Ure's mouth, "Shhhh. Don't say it. I know you believe me. You should believe me. I will leave him soon."

"You vomited again."

"I know. I hate myself every time but I can't be away from him. We need him."

"You don't."

She stands up. "When you're done, you will shave me. He wants it taken down." She chuckles, and then frowns. "Hurry, Ure. I must go see him tomorrow." She walks into the room.

***

I'm in this trailer-like room, skimming through my contact list. The familiar feeling has enveloped me again, this time, threatening to seal me in. I can only think to talk to someone-anyone. But the most I can do is flash them.

I want to cry but I know too well the foolishness of crying. It would only leave me hungrier and sap me of my remaining strength.

I'm in this cycle. I can't break free. Try as much as I want, I just cannot break free.

I know hopelessness.

It is walking back slowly to your house, knowing the only food you'll get for your hungry stomach is a human presence. It is the face of my mother and the veins that are constantly on the sides of her forehead. It is the creases on our clothes; we spend the night tossing from one side of the bed to another, dreaming, hoping. It is the compound we live in; where the excreta from the next compound seep lazily into ours like it has every right to. It is the room we live in, the room closest to the bathroom and toilet. It is the different sounds from there; of water splashing from human body to the ground; of the small pail tossed back into the bucket of bathing water; the sounds of farts and of people purging.

***

When you complain about your troubles to most people, they make examples of people who should be complaining but are not, all in a bid to give you hope. This was what Aunty did when I complained about our situation.

My Father left my Mother and I. I remember him selling everything he had, and leaving us with a twenty naira note. He promised to come back after making it big in life. That was fifteen years ago. I'm not sure I could pick him out in a crowd of few people. Maybe I could, for my Mother complains of how much of him she sees in me.

I wasn't supposed to fall for him. We were starving and I had to do something. I logged onto my 2go account and went straight to the romance room. Even though I wasn't looking for love, I couldn't go the flirting room. All the guys had to offer there were their dicks- their profile pictures were enough to attest to that.

He added me when I flipped the page to exit the room, and within minutes, we were talking like we had come a long way. A week later, he came to visit. A week after that, I went to visit.

After man twelve, I had learnt the art of playing naive when with a man. Men felt powerful when you trembled under their ministrations. What they wouldn't know is how you do it with two other men asides from them.

I trembled, I moaned, I arched, I fumbled, he was happy. I made my demands and we could eat that night.

I had never thought to cook for any man. But when I carried flasks every two weeks to see him, I knew I had fallen for him. I wasn't expecting to depend on a guy's call, but I depended on his. I especially loved the part when he called me with Igbo endearments. When I thought about the bad day I was having, I would remember his calls and smile. I could endure anything.

It wasn't long, I allowed him. Even when the pain was painful, I just lay there and bore it all.

It was love plus gratitude. He fed me and my Mother- he didn't know this by the way. And he saved me from being caned or sent out of the class- he bought every text I told him about.

A week later after we slept together, a month after we were not complaining of hunger and I realized I could take small cuts for him, he broke up with me. Dude claimed I was a distraction to him.

I thought I would die. But I didn't. I'm typing this.

You see, our different situations are peculiar. I don't think it right to compare a person's situation with another in a bid to give advice or hope. Most times these comparisons are not even related. An orphan has grown with the reality of no parents; I have a Mother and a Father. How can you compare these?

Weeks later, we were asked to leave the room we lived in. It was the same time I knew why Mother itched a lot. She had toilet infection that she hadn't treated in a year. By now, she was secreting blood and mucus; I saw her panties within the pile of clothes, at the back of the door. Hospital bills meant we wouldn't eat.

Mother tried. She worked even on the days she was sick. But try as she could, we were always broke.

After wracking every corner of her brain, Mother decided we would move to the village. This was after we swallowed our pride and asked Father for help. Uncle Chinedu, his brother, and the only relation we still conversed with from my Father's gave the number to us. But Father branded us, thieves and jobless people.

So, I thought, where better than run to a Church?

I ran to the Church and me was passed around from the Head Pastor to the tail Pastors.

I was numb. Then I felt pain later.

Then I learnt; I had to provide for myself, whatever I needed.

42

A lesson in mind, I cared for myself the only way I could.

***

Have you ever wondered how a person not close to you can sum up your life in a statement?

After swearing never to call again, I called my Father. After forcing myself to beg for money, he said to me, "You are hopeless."

People can just sum up your current disposition. I didn't have to look for a name for what I had become. It was hopeless.

I couldn't fight any more. I just did what I did.

No expectation, silenced regrets.

Many times, I think he is right.

***

Urenna places a bowl of water on the plastic table. She is Aunty's daughter- my aunty that now lives with my Mother. When I couldn't bear facing my Mother all the time, I packed into a room. Urenna was sent to stay with me since I was always providing.

 I spread my legs apart.

"Ure, take it easy oh."

"Okay."

The Writer

Sylvia Eguzoro is a third-year student of the department of Philosophy at the University of Nigeria, Nsukka. Adanne is her first short story. When she's not writing non-fiction, she's day-dreaming on weddings, shoes and plenty money.

Mobile: +2348188625091

Email: eguzoro77@gmail.com

Facebook: Sylvia Eguzoro

Aduala Bridge Final

by Ayodeji Isaac

HIGH COURT, IGBOSERE, 2001.

Special wasn't the word you'd use to describe Banjo. He was not one with an uncommon appearance, mannerism or any form of particularity that made him warrant a second glance from anybody. He could have passed for invincible but he had a body, an unspectacular sack of bones that hovered innocently in the periphery like a scentless fart, but was close enough to witness, in detailed terms, juicy happenings in whatever location he found himself. All these, coupled with the discomforting firmness of the cuffs clasping his wrists and the boxy dock, made the persistent glares from the gathering in the court murderous, like a knife held firmly against his throat.

The devil that led him there had deserted him since he'd told him to rob the bank.

ADUALA BRIDGE, 1993.

It was the first time he got a phone call from the devil. Banjo feared that he was insane as thirty minutes earlier, as he'd scuttled past a blind beggar seated on the pavement, trying hard to escape the choking fish smell wafting from her direction, he'd bumped her wizened outstretched arm. She strained her tired voice to call him a madman in Yoruba. And he could swear, almost immediately, he'd felt a slight jolt course through his body, like a small electric shock, followed by a brief spell of blankness, like his brain had begun the journey to degeneration.

Grum he heard.

It came with a vibration from the depth of his belly and an ache to his ears that forced him to his feet.

"It's me the devil." A voice said in the whispery tone haunted bedtime stories were told.

Banjo froze. "Devil ke?"

"I have a job for you," the voice began firmly, "Look to your right."

Banjo did and saw a young boy in a flabby grey suit strewn with wrinkles. There was a restrained persona about him; a scared look on his face, his eyes darting left and right at the faces of everybody that walked past him, the way a mouse looking to burst past a crowded parlour would.

"Go slap his face." The voice grunted

"Why?" Banjo asked, eyes still glued to the boy who began to pick his steps like the slightest misstep would see him swallowed beneath.

"Do it first and I will tell you later."

The boy stopped walking and looked up. His face was glistening with tears and his mouth, ugly and distorted like a gully, opened and closed repeatedly like an amateur actor trying too hard to portray grief. Banjo was overcome with fury. He didn't know why but as he watched the boy weep, he felt like snapping him like a twig, like putting a stop to an annoying irritation.

"You're wasting time." The voice said.

IKEJA UNDERBRIDGE, 1996.

The delectable smell of watermelon in a sea of fried palm oil speckled by the gracious black seeds of locust beans.

Grum.

It snapped Banjo out of a hunger inspired trance back into the scorching heat that was his reality. He'd been set to vanquish a steaming dish of Semovita and two large chicken wings when everything had gone black, a hissing sound had followed and then slowly, there'd been a warmth that intensified till he'd opened his eyes and realized he was back at the bridge, his reality where his last meal—if indeed it was a meal—was two days ago and it was one uninspiring cucumber he'd grabbed from a wool-gathering hawker.

Grum Grum, he heard again.

The last time he heard that was the day he was mobbed by a crowd for assaulting and trying to kidnap an innocent schoolboy. He would have been killed as he heard someone suggesting a tire and he could swear he'd seen a lighter out of the multitude of fisted hands and clubs, but policemen arrived at the nick of time and pulled him away. They'd taken him to a hospital where he was patched up and from there, dumped in the Kirikiri minimum prison that would be his home for four years. And all the while, there was no voice, but now it was back looking to land him in trouble again.

"What do you want this time?" Banjo asked through his clenched teeth.

"Look to your right…"

"I am not looking any right," Banjo interjected, "Leave me alone!"

"Then no food then."

"Yes, bye bye," Banjo said.

At the instant, the hunger tormenting him intensified so much that he felt a sharp pain in his belly that initiated a weakness and dizziness that very much felt like life was leaving him. Banjo finally turned to his right and saw a lady in a short black gown walking down the street, smiling and talking on the phone, a brown leather bag hanging on her forearm.

"The bag is open," the voice said, "Grab her purse."

Banjo looked around and saw how foolish the instruction was. There was a police van about three blocks away, three traffic wardens cramped in the rusty booth at the nearby junction, traders gaping red-eyed into space hoping for sales, and hoods hanging at corners, awaiting the next mugu to mug.

"Trust me." The voice said.

The sweet smell of watermelon soup brushed past his nose again and a gush of saliva obliterated the dryness in his mouth. He stopped walking and crossed the road, heading in the direction of the woman who was now digging frantically for something in her bag such that a significant portion of a red purse slanted outwards.

"I have made it easy now." The voice said.

IKEJA UNDERBRIDGE, 2001.

Change is that offspring of Mama Time that blankets every corner and every single thing, animate or otherwise. Except for Banjo. He remained exactly how he'd been five years ago when he got arrested: unspectacular and dull; a fleck of nothingness that happened to house a soul.

One sunny afternoon, Banjo was before the Ewa Agoyin seller thinking of how to plead for the burnt shards she had gathered into a steel bowl beneath her stand. He'd watched her insult a man who'd stretched a crisp 1000 naira note for not having change and he wondered, albeit a surge of pessimism, what the outcome would be if a beggar— who'd also been mistaken for a madman by some— attempted to transact. She'd probably chase him away with her big perforated spoon.

Grum grum.

Banjo immediately turned away and crossed to the other side of the road. There was no way he was listening to the voice of the devil. The same voice that had led him to jail twice. The voice would probably tell him to slap the woman and steal her pot of beans. It was the way of the voice, senseless and thoughtless.

"You better listen to me now." The voice said with urgency.

"I am not touching that—"

"Shut up and enter bus to Ojota." The voice interjected.

"Ojota? Why?"

"You want to die abi?" The voice said, "No problem then."

An unsettling silence followed. Then a soft howl of the breeze as it brushed against his skin, erupted goosebumps and sent shivers

48

all over his body. There was a tension in his chest, one that was supposed to accompany actual danger. Everything—humans and vehicles—seemed to be a tad slower.

"You are still looking?" the voice shouted.

Banjo ran to the nearby garage and jumped on a bus that was only two passengers away from filling up.

"Omo ake." The voice chuckled.

OJOTA, 2001.

Banjo wondered why the driver was yet to ask for payment. The closer and closer they bus got to the bus-stop, he concluded that the conductor had something nasty planned for him. He'd probably get grappled by the shirt or slapped and after the ensuing crowd have had their fill of free theatre, sympathetic persons would bail him out.

The moment the Ojota Bridge and the multitude navigating its narrow path was firmly in sight, Banjo took in a deep breath. The conductor whirled, finally focusing his intense reddened eyes on him after he'd repeatedly pretended he didn't exist as he collected money from the passengers minutes ago.

"You get change?" he asked in the typical hoarse voice of hoods.

Banjo shook his head quickly.

"I got your back bro." The voice said.

The bus screeched to a halt at the bus-stop and passengers were ordered to alight. Banjo hopped out of the bus expecting the bang but nothing came. As soon as his feet hit the ground, the bus sped away, coughing a black smoke that shaded his path.

"Jesus Christ!" A female voice screamed.

Banjo whirled and saw a woman in a fading Ankara gown wearing a grimace as she listened to someone over the phone. She suddenly pulled off her scarf with her free hand and flung it to the ground.

"Jesus no no no," she cried out loud, "Temi ba mi o. Olasunkanmi, don't leave me alone."

A crowd quickly gathered around her in time to stop her from throwing herself onto the ground.

"Kilosele?" One of them asked.

"Talk now." Another man shouted.

"Olasunkanmi ooo" She yelled again, tears slithering down her cheeks.

"Look at how she's shouting," the voice said. "All because her husband died."

"Ehn?" Banjo was puzzled.

"Oh yes, there was an explosion at Under bridge," the voice sighed. "I saved your life."

Banjo watched, traumatized, as some people from the crowd struggled to drag the phone from her hands. She fought hard, tightening her grip so many veins laced her forehead like webs but she eventually let go and resumed her yelling, insistent on falling to the ground, perhaps to roll.

"Let me die!" She shouted flailing her hands in the air.

Banjo walked away, unable to bear the sight of pain wrangling her sanity to submission. He mounted the bridge and began to think of his next destination, somewhere he could get food or a means to get food, a job perhaps, probably a bricklayer. He'd rejected several offers to work as a labourer at construction sites; those were the early days he'd foolishly thought the stringency a necessary steep slope to negotiate before some form of success not knowing it was life itself.

"There's a bank at the other side of the bridge." The voice whispered.

HIGH COURT, IGBOSERE, 2001.

"Does the defendant have anything to say?" The judge asked in a deep voice that pierced the silence.

Banjo shook his head.

Murmurs suddenly filled the courthouse. Banjo looked down, trying hard to avoid the glares. The husky smell of dried sweat from his pits coursed into his nose. He shook his head lightly.

"Order! court!" The judge roared as he slammed his anvil again and again. Silence cloaked the gathering once again.

"Why did you kill the security man?" The judge asked.

"Hellfire isn't that bad." The voice whispered, "Don't listen to the revelations."

"Leave me alone," Banjo shouted.

"Excuse me?" The judge retorted as he took off his glasses.

The silence in the house pulsated in tension.

"I wasn't talking to you," Banjo grumbled

Murmurs filled the courthouse again.

"Order!" The judge shouted, before lowering his voice to ask "Who were you talking to?"

"The devil."

A glow came upon the face of the judge, a childish smirk of some sort that reeked of mischief. "What was he saying?" he asked.

"That I am going to hellfire."

Laughter filled the building. Even the Judge covered his obvious amusement with his fat hands for a moment before recovering to slam his anvil. Decorum returned gradually but murmurs persisted in the background.

"I better hurry with my judgement then," The judge said smiling. "We don't want to keep the devil waiting."

THE END.

The Writer

Isaac is a physiotherapist by day, a reader by night, and writer every second. He is currently working on a festival-bait short film with his budding filmmaking company. He hopes his hands so adept as manipulation and rehabilitation can mould tales worthy of remembrance and rehashing.

Mobile: +234 9051448124

Email: seyisicinc1994@gmail.com

Facebook: Ayodeji Oluwaseyi Isaac

Instagram: oi ayodeji

Ashawo

by Abiodun Opeyemi Awodele

Dawn is not the best time to visit Charity Hotel. If visited at that time of the day for whatever reasons, what you would see is a lie. You see peace and quiet, you see emptiness, and you will come to a conclusion, a wrong one.

Hotel Charity at dawn is an unrecognizably calm kettle of fish, a world of difference from the dimly lit cauldron of nefarious human activity it is at night. The main hall is a shell, with plastic chairs and tables scattered around, many of them overturned and left that way by revellers. The pockmarked cement floor is littered with all sorts - cigarette butts, empty bottles, bottle caps and crumpled plastic cups – testament to the orgy of consumption that was the night before. The silence is profound, as the two giant speakers responsible for booming out musical noise quietly recline in their corners, now ordinary wooden boxes in the absence of their earphone wearing puppet master, DJ Sabinus.

The regular troupe of garishly painted and scantily clad working girls is out of sight, in their rooms, slumbering in different beds as they recover from the exertions of the previous night. All the customers have crawled back to their different holes save for one or two prime callers who have a special status that allows them to pass the night on the premises whenever they choose to.

Dawn meets everything and everyone in Charity Hotel recovering from the frenetic flexing of the night, just a few hours before they emerge from their different caves with batteries fully recharged, ready to begin preparations for yet another night of debauchery.

It is a cycle of life that never ends.

I'm an early riser, a habit I never appreciated until I got here. Regardless of how late I sleep at night or how tired I am when I hit the bed, my internal alarm wakes me up on the dot of five. It

53

is a legacy of my days at home. For anybody born of a woman who happens to sleep under my mother's roof, only death or ill health can excuse your being in bed after the devotion bell rings at five in the morning. If you were not dead or indisposed and tarried a-bed after that bell goes, mama would find you, and her wake-up slap would make you wish you were either of the two. The worst part of it was that after prayers which were led by papa and usually dragged on for at least an hour, morning chores would immediately follow, so there was no chance at all for bleary eyes to find a few minutes of reprieve before the sun came up and it was time for school.

I used to hate being up so early. These days, however, I like waking up before the other inmates of Charity Hotel. I like the quietude, the freedom to lie peacefully in bed while different thoughts silently rush through my head. Dawn is the only time of day when you can listen to your own mind in this mad place.

On some days I would just curl up in my bed and read; a second -hand novel someone left behind, a magazine, an old newspaper, anything at all. Reading is another habit born of my mother's influence that has refused to die. Once in a while when I lacked any other material, I would even read some verses from the Holy Bible, although that book no longer holds any special significance for me.

Today, memories of my mother roam in my head as it rests on the pillow I fashioned myself from a few of my old wrappers. Electricity is out as usual and the generator has been shut down, so as I lie on my back, torch in hand, staring at the stained plywood ceiling, I try to picture mama standing right in the centre of this room.

As hard as I try, the image doesn't fit.

The mother I remember would rather die. Everything here would kill her, and quickly too. How will it be possible that my own mother, Deaconess Adanna Nkem Osotule, will miraculously find herself in an ashawo's room where unmarried people copulate, right inside a den of iniquity where Lucifer's children

54

gather to frolic without any feelings of shame or restraint and not give up the ghost?

Impossible!

Imagine mama, standing in front of the partially torn and dirt smeared poster of a naked Kim Kardashian on the wall, looking at all my skimpy clothes and flimsy undies draped on the wall hanger, or catching a glimpse of the open red plastic chamberpot in the corner which is overflowing with swollen condoms carrying the slowly dying seeds of yesterday's customers. Tufia! Even her corpse would awaken, jump up and run outside if you brought it here to lie in state. She's probably fuming at me in heaven for even daring the thought.

Sex was always a taboo best avoided as far my mother was concerned during her lifetime. She would shut down any discussion remotely concerned with the topic. I remember the day I came home, fresh from Integrated Science class and full of questions about the workings of the female body and menstruation. Mama almost slapped me before she dumped her battle-worn bible on my laps and told me to read an entire chapter of the Psalms. Her faith in God was too strong for such human trivialities.

Once I saw her hurriedly make a sign of the cross at the sight of two dogs mating in the street on our way to the market before turning away to find another route. Of course, I pretended I didn't know why we chose another path, and I didn't ask. I used to wonder how she got married to papa and why, how it was that they managed to have me if sex was such an oddity. The answers, unfortunately, came too late.

That was how my father surreptitiously slipped into my thoughts. Prophet Chuma Nathaniel Osotule. It is virtually impossible to remember the man without his bushy beard, which is funny, because before his illness he liked to shave clean every morning, and sometimes even twice in a single day. The damn thing only gained life after the debilitating stroke which left half his body useless. He and his beard became an illustration of contrasting fortunes, because as one grew frail, so did the other become more luxuriant.

That stroke had been the answer to my many nights of whispered prayers, prayers fearfully and hastily murmured as I lay in bed every night listening for footsteps which I knew would come. They never failed. From the first night when he forcefully took my maidenhead after mama passed. Just after I turned fourteen. The fateful night he fell like a log outside the main door, he never stopped coming after. Even when my period was on he would force his turgid flesh into my hands and mouth until he found relief. Afterward, while watching as I cleaned off his slime he would repeat the harsh mantra he always silenced me with.

"Tell anybody about this and I will kill you."

There was always that light in his eyes when he said it, the same light that danced in his eyes when he delivered a sermon on Sundays at the Christ Is Coming to Pentecostal Ministries where he was a god. Hypnotized by that light, the congregation nodded and swallowed every word that came out of his holy mouth. I did too until the stroke called his bluff.

Some other times his tone would be softer, almost apologetic, as he explained how years of sexual starvation by mama had forced him into towing this perverted version of parenthood. It was during one of those sessions I learned how he had fornicated with mama as a virgin Sunday school teacher and she was his student. I was the result of that one error of judgment, and mama had turned to 'God' immediately her folly became known. Yes, they were hastily wedded to save both of them from shame, but sex was off the menu for most of the union according to him. A part of me thinks both of them hated me in their own individual ways for how things turned out. Mama, because I reminded her of the one time she fell from grace and Papa because I was like the trigger that consigned him to marital purgatory. He usually narrated the story like it should make me understand as if it would ease my pain or erase the wretched way I felt about me.

At some point before his death, his beard used to be the only thing I could see from the door when I peeped in to check if he was still with us. I only went entered his room twice every day, when I took his food and cleaned him up. The morning he died, I thought I was free because the bush attached to his jaw had finally stopped stirring.

What I didn't know then, was that I would never be.

Ashawo – Prostitute

The Writer

Abiodun 'Maskuraid' Awodele lives in Lagos and writes both fiction and poetry. His e-book 'Always & Forever' was recently published and is available for sale on Amazon, Play Store and iBooks. He blogs at www.versesbybeordoon.com.

Mobile: +2348055209179

Email: beordoon@gmail.com

Twitter: @maskuraid

Instagram: @maskuraid

Book of Goals

by Kayode Bukunmi Sonibare

I stood by the slightly open window of my father's bungalow, peeping at a procession of the kingmakers, the new king and the oracle diviners whose figures were barely visible to my eyes. It was past midnight, and the moon had refused to rise from behind the clouds. I knew it was a taboo for women and girls to view the midnight procession, it was a tradition I had known since childhood, but I was eager nonetheless to take a peek through the window.

"This isn't the first tradition you've broken away from after all," I whispered to myself with a sense of self-guilt lodged amidst courage.

I sensed someone had turned to look in the direction of the window and I instantly crouched by the window; my heart pounding and my hand firmly gripping the wall made of mud; plastered and painted blue. I listened carefully to the moving procession and focused my ears on the sound of anyone approaching the window. I crouched by the window until I was convinced there was no one approaching. I slowly tiptoed to the bed in the room and laid beside my husband under a big blanket. I closed my eyes almost immediately but stayed awake for several minutes as my mind slowly drifted to the words of the chief priest during a pre-coronation ceremony held in full view of all villagers by the bank of the village river. There, the spirit of the river goddess was called upon to lend its support to the new king and bless his reign.

I stood under a big tree on the upper grounds from where I watched the ceremony with my husband by my side. My husband is not a native of my village and so he insisted that we watched from the upper grounds. We watched as the chief priest sprinkled a liquid concoction into the river, recited some incantations and said prayers for the new king and the villagers. Though the king was absent as was required by tradition, the people enthusiastically danced in front of the river goddess's shrine and they all chorused 'ase' to each prayer said by the chief priest. No one apart from my husband and I had their mouths sealed throughout the ceremony. For us, it was more like tourism and so we drew the wrath of my mother who berated us for merely looking like sheer spectators. She moved closer to me and whispered harshly that my actions were no different from that of a stranger. I refused to mind her words and pretended not to hear her clearly while the chief priest reeled out warnings to girls and women.

"No woman and no girl must come out tonight when the new king goes to consult the spirits of his predecessors." The old man shouted on top of his voice.

"Ancestral spirits will be out on our streets by midnight and they will strike any woman or girl who dares to see them."

Those words had reverberated in my ears before I tried looking out the window to view the procession in disobedience to the chief priest's warning. I could hear them loudly again in my ears and I waited for an instant judgement from the gods. I waited for what could have been an hour before I concluded I had not violated the chief priest's warning or that he had fooled us all at the ceremony.

I woke up the next morning, not sure of when sleep swept me into its solemn arms. My husband was awake at the time, crosschecking my notes for the speech which I was to deliver at the king's coronation the next day. The new king had walked into my chamber in Lagos three weeks before and had insisted I deliver a speech at his coronation. I was his closest classmate during our primary school years and had grown to be his favourite human rights lawyer. My husband threw me a puzzled look when I tapped his back, he pointed to the paper in his hand and made to read out part of my prepared speech.

"I respect our traditions though many might think otherwise. I hear gossips at the village market, that I'm strong willed and refuse to uphold traditions." He began to read out.

"Every society has good and bad traditions and none has a perfect set of mores. After over a decade of living in a renowned city and my escapades outside the shores of our country, there are many of our traditions that I now cherish more than I did when I lived here.

Here, we respect our elders, we care for our aged ones, we live as communal families, our daughters can inherit properties and we don't discriminate against our girls going to schools. Those are few which I can remember. And as much as I do not think a day like this should receive highlights of some of our traditions which I abhor; whenever I go to visit my gynaecologist, I think of our village and I hold the elders of this village, my parents and an evil tradition as responsible for some of my pains.

When ignorance reigns, pain and anguish are inevitable. Some of the pains I experience while I perform my matrimonial duty, during childbirth and others which I'll hold back, are as a result of the mutilation, which many of us know as circumcision, carried out on me at childhood. I did my research and found out that some of the infections, pains and difficulties which our girls and women experience especially in their sexual organs are results of circumcising our girls.

Our ancestors began this practice to reduce the sexual urge of our girls and ensure they are virgins until they marry. Their intention to curb sexual immorality is good but the practice is unhealthy to our girls and it deprives them of fully experiencing the desire for sex even in marriage. We celebrate this tradition because we care about our girls' virginity but how about we also show care to our boys' virginity. Girls lose their virginity to men and it will only be fair to teach both our boys and girls to be sexually pure. Our girls can heed our calls for sexual chastity without trying to take away or reducing their God-given desire

60

for sex. Today, I stand to call this tradition evil and say it must stop."

My husband expressed his reservations that morning, stating the hazards to antagonizing traditions. I looked into his eyes which stared bewildered as I read out the speech at the coronation. I quickly turned from him and set my eyes on some village elders who furiously gawked at me. In the crowd, I saw a man whispering to some youths and I immediately brought my eyes to those of the new king. The king's mien was calm and rather reassuring, and so I continued, asserting my stance on female gender mutilation before moving on to speak on other issues.

Immediately I concluded my speech and returned to my seat, a man in black suit and sunglasses, one of the kings' personal security officers, approached me and led me out to a black tinted jeep. I hopped into the jeep following his orders and met my husband already seated with our two kids.

"What's happening?" I asked my husband.

"The king ordered we leave immediately. He fears for our safety because your speech angered the villagers," my husband replied.

I felt quite ashamed of myself for jeopardizing the safety of my family and quickly drew close my kids and assured them we would be safe. We journeyed from the village square towards the outskirts till we approached the village border where fierce looking young men brandished cutlasses and charms. I suddenly felt my heart slipping out of my chest. Fear gripped my whole being as we advanced towards them and it did not subside until we drove past them. Apparently, they recognized the king's jeep and allowed us to go through the border without asking any questions. Instead, they hailed us with praises and even saluted us.

Suddenly, the king's driver increased his speed on the rough road after taking a turning to the right. His driving was rough and the speed was high. We complained and whined but all fell on deaf ears. He refused to respond to our pleas until my husband threatened to forcefully stop him.

61

"Madam, the chiefs and priests want you arrested and they would have sent the village guards after us," he eventually responded.

"We all are not safe if they meet us here and besides, our journey is still long as I am taking you to Lagos."

And so, we arrived Lagos three hours later. My husband trudged into our apartment droning in anger at me for risking our lives and those of my family in the village. He recollected an incidence that occurred the previous day at the house of my younger brother, fuming as he did.

***

I was with my younger brother's wife when one of the village midwives arrived to circumcise her three months old daughter to which I refused vehemently. My younger brother was angry at me but had little to say because he respected me and thought I was the smart child of our father. He did nothing like our some of our relatives, his friends and some nearby villagers thronged his house and insisted on the circumcision. They said it was a taboo for a girl child not to be circumcised and they called me the crazy one who wanted to bring disrepute to an age long tradition. I left my brother's house irately and made up my mind to speak against the tradition at the coronation the next day. After all, I had already broken away from the tradition by not circumcising my daughter who was five years old.

***

My husband and I later retired to bed after he had recalled the incidence and rebuked me for risking our lives. He took to his side of the bed, choosing to look at the wall by his side.

"Darling," I called.

"It's the king calling," I whirred.

He sprung up to sit on the bed and requested we both listen to the king through an earpiece.

"Moladun," the king called me by my first name.

"I salute your bravery," he continued rather slowly.

62

"I heard of the incidence at your brother's house and with the Moladun that I've come to know, I was not surprised by your call to end female genital mutilation. I knew your speech would include something or more on human rights and I'm happy at your choice. You have once again dared tradition. When we were young, you did the unthinkable by playing the flute at the village square. You also surprised all when you followed your father on hunting escapades as a teenager. I always saw the rebel in you. I advise you tread carefully as I've always told you and I assure to end female genital mutilation as you requested of me."

I felt a sudden flush of excitement at the king's words. I saluted him, paid him homage and requested for the protection of my family at the village.

"I assure you of their safety," he responded.

"Greetings to your husband and children."

My husband drew me into his arms after the call and kissed me on my lips.

"You know am proud of you," he crooned.

"And I'll always stand by you."

He jumped out of bed and brought out my 'Book of Goals' from the desk drawer in our room.

"I'm pretty sure that 'goal' is somewhere in this book," he said to me grinning loudly.

"Now tick it. I'm sure it's achieved."

I did as was requested and we both tittered playfully.

The Writer

Kayode is an aspiring writer with a passion for mirroring societal intricacies and creating imaginative stories. He is an ardent lover of football, movies and 'good' music; and he has a heart for teaching, freelance writing and quality control. He is a graduate of Obafemi Awolowo University and a fabulous sound engineer.

Mobile: +2348148311545

Email: sonibuk@gmail.com

Facebook: Sonibare Kayode Sho

Instagram: @kaysoni

Twitter: @sonibarekayode

LinkedIn: Sonibare Kayode

Broken

by Paul Bobsyn Utibeh

You lie on your back quietly, staring at the ceiling. The memories come rushing back and you squint like you've been caught off guard by a powerful ray of light. Many different thoughts race through your head as you stroke your forehead tenderly. You were quickly materializing into your worst fears and it scared you. You can't make a head or tail of how you've lived with the guilt for so long but you know why. You are aware of your oratorical proficiency and how it gets you out of trouble. Your extremely complicated personality which makes it almost impossible for people to smell rats on you is also not new to you.

You toss on the bed as the memories hit you one at a time, slowly, making their marks. Your eyes dart to the clock on the wall which strikes midnight almost immediately. The sound of snoring filters from your sibling's room into yours and you can tell he had no problem falling asleep. You're not susceptible to insomnia, but somehow, those memories exist to keep your eyes open all night long. You try reliving the bliss of the full night rest you had the day before but your restless mind can't focus and you're soon thinking about other things and trying vainly to refocus again. Frustrated, you give up.

Somehow, you'd make more of those memories in the morning and again at night, they'd come to haunt you. You feel caught in your very own trap and you're at a loss on how again to regain freedom. Tears run down your cheeks onto the pillows on which you rest your head and your sighs pierce the stillness of the night. You would do it tonight; try to face your fears; but as much as you feel unprepared, you decide to put an end to it regardless.

As you shut your eyes, stifling your cries to avoid waking anyone, your eyelids quiver slightly and you grab a fistful of the blanket that covers you. It doesn't take long for the memories to roll in and begin all over again. The scene of the previous day pops up. Your mom had asked for your help with the dishes but you'd turned her down. "I do all the work around here," you'd said, "you should do some too." Tears glistened in her eyes, you saw it and you knew she'd cry in the solace of her room afterwards. She's done enough raising you and your brother since your father's demise, you know, heaven knows, but somehow you feel she overworks you. Like all truths, it's a bitter pill to swallow, and avowing to being wrong isn't your strong point.

You wonder why you'd been hard on your mom and treated her so. You can't make out any reasonable excuse for your overbearing attitude and your conscience pricks you sore. You tell yourself to apologise by morning but you're unsure of yourself. When sober, your ego would prove a big enough inhibition and you'd overlook all your reconsiderations of the previous night. After she'd bade you and your brother goodnight and retired to her room, you'd tiptoed to her door to eavesdrop on her. You heard her sob lightly in her prayers, she was on her knees, you saw her through the keyhole. Her prayers were what broke you; she'd prayed for your success irrespective of how unruly you'd become. You'd returned to your room stunned, unspeaking. You just couldn't fathom the love she had for you. The same love that purged you now, bringing to light the memories you long had buried in the asylum of your stony heart. Haunted by these memories; of hurt people had suffered by you; you'd stumbled into bed.

Another memory succeeds the first quickly. You recall the scene vividly although you can't remember the date exactly. You and a couple of friends had been at your neighbour's shop when the electric power came on. Slowly, everyone had left for their houses leaving just you and the shop owner behind. You were about leaving when she'd asked you to help watch over her shop while she went to urinate. You recall the last time she'd said that when there was power. She'd returned minutes later after watching a program on TV, much to your contempt. You saw an opportunity for a comeback and grabbed it with eager hands.

66

Never again would you fall for the same trick, you told yourself. You disagreed and disappeared between the gates in a flash.

In your haste, you saw her face fall. When in the confines of your room, you felt bad about your actions and dashed back out with a naira bill you retrieved from your bag. She's not in the shop when you returned and you seated yourself, cooking up a good enough excuse to tell her. She finally showed up and you saw tears well in her eyes. She'd relate your actions to her childlessness, you knew and braced yourself. In a grieving voice, she'd said you'd deserted her. Your oratorical skills kicked in and you stopped her midway before she brought up the subject of her barrenness. You showed her the one hundred naira note in your hands, telling her you were kidding and had only gone to get your money.

Although you had no appetite for sugary food, you purchased a wafer and sachet water in hopes of looking justified. She looked like she'd accepted your excuse and handed you your change. Again, you vanished through the gates, a mixture of indifference and freedom settling over you. As you whimper now, you think. Perhaps she'd cried that night, wetting her pillow just as you did now, reminding the Great-He of his promises, all the while remembering the stunt you pulled on her. A sigh escapes your lips and your vision is blurred by tears as you roll onto your side, leaving a dark wet patch on your pillow.

Again, another memory succeeds the latter. You recall the very moment with a fresh flow of sobs. Pondering over how foolish and selfish and unthinking you had been. You want to pull at your hair and inflict pain on yourself but your hands lie limp, unmoving. Cecily had been a friend long before you attended the university. You met her online and when you finally met in school, things had taken shape and a new turn. Your chats were frequent and you both had warmed up to each other. Then came the fateful day; the day she chose to ask that serious question, the day your policies meddled in your life because you couldn't keep your fingers in situ and your thoughts to yourself.

67

She'd called you a friend and you'd called her an acquaintance. Time had stood still when you both came to see each other's perspective. She was hurt and had said goodnight afterwards. You ought to have apologized or offer soothing words, you know you should've, but you didn't. You can't say for sure what stopped you; your ego or apathy. You said your byes and went offline. A later discovery showed she'd read your message and was still online even after you left. You juxtaposed her feelings with how you'd have felt, putting yourself in her shoes. You can't take the pain realization brings upon you and peeling back the blanket, you scuttle to your feet.

Walking through the moonlit passage to the parlour, you feel weary and your feet drag with reluctance along the floor. Your head isn't yours anymore as you walk, what with the many different thoughts that leave you questioning whether you deserve to see the light of another day. When you get to the parlour, you see your mom sitting on the couch reading a bible by the light of a bedside lamp. As you examine her sitting figure, you recall the once young and vibrant woman she'd been until your father's death and fresh tears brim in your eyes. Your father's death had dealt her a devastating blow, crippled her even and it's a miracle she survived it.

You're repentant remembering her unwavering love which only increased towards you and your sibling on a daily basis. You sniff and she looks up from the bible at you. You run to her, falling at her feet, wounding your arms around her, crying. Your lips part to let out those bittersweet words but words elude you and you could only mouth it to her — "I'm sorry." She nods and the tears in her eyes catch the lamp's light. Her strength fills you and you feel your grief ebbed away slowly as she strokes your back softly.

Her tears fall on your face and you feel washed anew, bereft of the pain of the memories that'd driven you to seek solace. It

68

doesn't take long before you fall asleep on her laps under the ministrations of her gentle and reassuring pats. She wipes your tearstained face with her palms and smile at your sleeping figure. By morning you would wake up in your bed, happy, loved, a changed person.

The Writer

Paul Bobsyn otherwise known by his diminutive, Porl Bob Jnr, is an avid reader and freelance writer who when not being an overly sarcastic twit is almost always behind a screen doing what he does best — learning.

Mobile: +2348138340686

Email: phemmygoldjr@gmail.com

Facebook: Porl Bob Jnr

Buried in Time

by Akinyemi Muhammed A

Memories of you are buried deep in my head like rocks into soil, firmly, and with no definiteness as to when it was planted – the rocks in the soil, your memories in my head. Even more, buried, are the emotions I feel for you, clad in regard and unreciprocated love. I have taken pills of depressants to fight the ailment the thought of you brings to my heart. The more pills I took, the harder I loved and wanted to be adequate enough, just for you.

How little words can tear deep into our memories, exterminating the beautiful memories we made, I will never know. I grew in your eyes, and under what I thought was love. The sands we played with and the memories buried beneath them; the horses we mounted and the galloping pain that followed; the see-saw of happy times, and the never stopping merry-go-round of pain that cycled afterwards; all that could have been memories to hold on to, fell like the biblical Goliath before David.

***

We were happy together. For a long time, everything seemed perfect; little did I know those times were the calm before the storm. Young as I was, I would eat from your hand, and you mine. We would sit and watch the sunset. On some days when you visited, your face would be as dry as a desert, laced with grains of hidden pain and hard work, behind an oasis of joy that was buried in your eyes. On days you came back sweaty; I would wipe your forehead with my cloth and sing to you. Mother had a habit of beating me for wiping your sweat with my shirt until she got tired. But it was always worth it; watching as your face transformed from a wet, worried, anguished form to a dry, full-of-expectations, happy one. I always admired the transformation. We buried seeds of fruits and waited for them to grow. Most of those seeds came out well, but with them came a tree of displeasure, and an apple of discord that settled on your soil – our soil.

Soils reminded me of your skin. How you could be dark in a week, looking red at times, and white on rare moments, but mostly brown. Your heart, mind, and body were engaged too much with not letting your father down that you cared less what you looked like, as long as I was happy with you, and he too.

On some days, the wind blows joy, dreams, and love, on some days, the air carries heartbreak, disappointment, and broken dreams. On one of such bad days, you had asked me, "what would you like to do when you grow up?" and I had replied "write about us." Showing my almost brown dentition as I said it, hoping to be embraced by your smile, but I had met a scowl accompanied by a reprimanding expression on your face. I could swear you wanted to hit me, but you couldn't. You weren't in the position to. Mother would never allow me to see you again. Not that she liked you being around anyway. "That big sack of weakness" she had said when I asked why she didn't like you much. You wanted me to be a lawyer. To grow up and wear suits, while telling men and women under wigs and cloaks why I think a particular rich man deserves to breathe, be granted sick leave so they can spend funds embezzled from the government. In all your scenarios of what a lawyer was, you never for once mentioned a poor man, or woman, who needed my defence. They were always about expatriates, politicians, and plainly successful people. "It's a boring life" – from the moment I told you, and I needed no arbitrator to tell me things were no longer at ease. "You want to grow up poor, complaining about failed book sales and little promotions? Talking about friends earning better for lesser work? Going home with more complains than money? Do you want to build a home that way? How will you see your parents as a writer? You would go to your mother and beg for clothes, and your father to beg for will? A writer is poor. Please be a lawyer, apple of my eyes."

I was broken by your words for many reasons. I thought you shared my dreams, I thought despite the different bed sheets and roofs that we lay under, we still saw the same dreams. But I was determined to write about us; even if they were sad tales. I sat in my room one day watching as the evening air carried away our memories while mother told you at the door that I didn't want to see you. I cried over it as you walked away. Your short, black hair would wave to me and my tears would wave back. "Your love would not be the reason my ambition would be abandoned" I consoled myself.

***

I went ahead to study writing as a discipline. I was told of how you severally came looking for me, of how you came knocking and begging my mum to not let me grow up poor. But my resolve was tight, with no gap for weakness, just like your dentition. I wanted to show you, to tell you, to let you know that a writer could be rich, successful, and not have to worry about book sales. I was ready to show you that I would weather the greatest of tempests as if I were Poseidon, and come out unscathed.

Mother would tell me about you, about the disappointments you felt. Mother would surprisingly ask me if I thought I was doing the right thing, and if I wasn't too harsh on you, but I would say "no. my head knows better than my heart." I heard you wouldn't stop fighting too; that you wouldn't stop running in pursuit of your father's happiness. In keeping the name, your father had worked for, and his father before him. But I was different. You had told me this yourself. "You're a special channel of different energy," your eyes had glistened as you told me this. You had been honest when you said the words.

***

I had heard you lost your father. I had buried all the indifference I built on the memories of your wishes for me, to come and pay my regards. But it had taken the power of all five of your siblings to stop you from hitting me. I remember telling you as I left, head tucked in the ground like a dog casted away by its owner, that I love you. I had meant it, every bit of the sentence. But you would

72

say to me, "You're inadequate and undeserving of my affections." I wouldn't ache more than I already had. I would only spend a long time telling myself I was undeserving of your affection. And I would never look back.

***

"I want to dedicate this award to my father. Because of him, I have made you all bleed through your eyes, at a time or another... and to laugh too. More than he knows it, he has been my motivation"

I stepped off the podium, teary eyed and heartbroken than I ever was. My handkerchief became soiled with the only expression of my heartbreak – my tears – as I made it out of the exquisite attention of the hall. "Best writer of creative fiction," the award in my hand read. As prestigious as the award made me, I still felt emptiness. My wife understood this in the car as we drove home, my mother in the backseat in her unspoken words grieved with me, but everyone else only cared about the smile before the camera. A wise man had once said, "Smile for the camera, die silently after. It's what keeps the market going." Was I that wise man in one of my many books? I wouldn't know. The same way I wouldn't know how father felt hearing about my many successes. He had told me he loved to read newspapers; I have tried to picture his expression when he would read that I had become a Nobel Prize for literature winner. But memories of him were faint. As faint as the colours of my hair that had lost the blackness it carried in youth. The hair that reminded me of yours, as you walked out that day, when mother had told you I didn't want to see you.

For years I would try to understand why you had impregnated mum, knowing well that your father – the one I only saw only on his obituary posters – would not allow you marry her. I would never know why you would treat mum like a stranger every time you visited, while giving me all of your love. I would never be able to tell why you wanted me to be a lawyer so desperately. But what I would forever remember were your words, "You're inadequate and undeserving of my affections."

Perhaps I could say the same of you now too.

The Writer

Akinyemi Muhammed A, is a Nigerian poet and story teller who writes under the pseudonym, Princely X. He is the author of a short story collection titled Broken Arrows, which is available for purchase on CFWRITERZ.COM store. He is a first runner up at Designed life catalyst contest, amongst other many performances. He has a few writing awards and recognitions to his name.

Mobile: +2348177522712

Email: akinyemimuhammed@gmail.com

Facebook: Akinyemi Princely X Adedeji

Instagram: @princely_x

Twitter: @theprincelyx

74

EkiOba

by Erhu Amreyan

We used to live in one of those houses in Aduwawa built by the government for civil servants. Such houses were easily identified by the rusted corrugated roof worn out over time by the occasional rain and blistering sun that was characteristic of Benin City. It had one bedroom, a parlor, a kitchen and a bathroom I was sure had never seen running water. Hence it was my duty to use jerry cans to fetch water from our neighbor's house to fill the two giant drums occupying the greater part of the kitchen. I disliked the task so much. Carrying jerry cans in a rickety wheelbarrow everyday was no easy task.

But we could not afford to live in a fancier house. My father who worked in a brewery and my mother who was a petty trader selling cray fish and ogbonor seeds were scraping by to provide for their three children.

My older sister Mirabel who had just entered secondary school needed new books and my little sister Osas, who was still a baby fell sick so often she needed to be hospitalized. Mirabel tried to explain when I asked her why. She only ended up confusing me. All I could grasp from her was Osas was an SS which prompted the her to fall sick all the time.

I was just about to turn eight when tragedy struck my family. It was around the time harmattan came early and schools were closed for the holiday.

I had woken up early that day to help my mother tie up her wares into a sack. My father had already left before anyone stirred from sleep. He was a hard worker my father and he was never late for anything.

My mother dished out a few orders for Mirabel as she strapped Osas on her back with a blue worn out wrapper.

'Ehigie,' she called me.

'Ma,' I answered.

'Don't drag food with your sister. Make sure you take whatever she gives you.' I nodded and smiled mischievously. 'I'm going,' she said picking up the sack which she hoisted up on her head with no effort. She walked briskly toward the main road where she would take a taxi to Oba market in Ring Road. There she would sell her wares before coming back home to prepare the evening food.

After we ate breakfast, my sister and I went outside and waited on the broken front steps. Our house was one of the headquarters for other children in the street to come around to play. We usually played suwe, game box, whot or hide and seek. Soon enough five of them trooped to the house and asked what game we would play. We chose suwe but when other children began to arrive we decided on game box.

'I challenge you to choose' my sister said to another girl with their little fingers interlocked.

'I cut,' the other girl said using her free hand to unlock their fingers. With that they both chose who would be on their team. I ended up in the team of the other girl. We drew the box on the ground and positioned our teammates where we wanted. The game went on for a few minutes before someone shouted. 'Den don bring light! NEPA!' There was a loud uproar from all of us because we all knew what that meant. It was time for Power Rangers.

My father who could not afford to buy DSTV or any cable at all resorted to buying a fairly used DVD player. He then bought alongside it a collection of Power Rangers movies. The DVD player constantly gave us problems where we had to tap it to get it working again and the graphics of the movie was nothing short of a blur but we loved it; from the costumes to the silly robots the rangers fought, we enjoyed every bit of it. Everyone took their places in the parlor and waited for the movie to start.

'Has it started yet?' Igho asked rushing in through the front door. Igho was a boy who lived at the end of our street and my classmate in school. I did not like Igho. Not one bit. The boy was known for his long throat and gorimapa head. He always knew the exact times to come to my house so that my food will be shared with him. I wanted him to go away. Since his father could not buy him power rangers, he should not come to my house to watch it. I could not tell him that because if I did, Mirabel would tell our mother and she would beat me, telling me to be more like young Jesus in the Bible.

Igho sat on the ground next to me and folded his legs. When the screen lit up with the colorful images, we all shouted in glee. About thirty minutes into watching we all heard a shrill ringing noise. It was coming from the bathroom.

'Mummy's phone.' Mirabel said running out of the parlor. She could be heard talking to someone on the phone. After she ended the call she walked back to announce that she had to put off the television.

'Mummy said we should come and give her phone.'

'Can't you go alone?' I asked thinking of the movie I would miss.

'No.'

'You know NEPA will take the light eh Mirabel. When will we watch Power Rangers?'

'When there is light again. Just get up from there.'

Mirabel put off the television and told everyone we were going out. Within five minutes, the house was empty and Mirabel and I were on our way to the market. We did not wait long by the roadside before we found a taxi heading toward Ring Road. I had to sit on Mirabel's lap to save transport fare. We sat in between a Hausa man who smelled like burnt goat and a woman who bared her breast to feed her hungry child.

The driver who had on his radio nodded as the voice coming from it spoke at length about the dangers of letting anger control the actions of men.

'This is what my pastor was talking about on Sunday. No matter how angry you are you should control yourself. So many wahala have started because of anger. Onigbese that is not your own, you will now carry it on top of your head.'

It was the driver who was now preaching to us. I tried to listen with effort to the man on the radio who was broadcasting from the National Television Authority station. What he was saying sounded more interesting than the driver's. As we flowed with the traffic in Ramat Park, another car coming from Agbor road bumped into our taxi. Both cars came to a screeching halt. The other driver came out of his car to access the damage on it and so did our driver. Instead of the other man to apologize, he began throwing insults at our driver for driving like an epileptic patient.

Mirabel told us to get down and take another taxi. I looked back on the driver who was not saying anything to the shouting man and wondered how badly he was trying to control his anger.

We found a bus heading in our direction and entered it. Nothing eventful happened on our way except for the conductor occasionally opening the door to let people in and out. We got down by the banks in Ring road and walked toward Oba market all the while dodging the crowd of buyers and sellers.

'Fine girl you no want jeans?' One of the sellers said to my sister. 'Stock jeans for shekele money.'

Mirabel frowned and hissed at the man. She took my hand as we crossed the road toward the markets. We did not have to walk for long before seeing our mother under a huge umbrella. Her ogbonor were laid out in a table in front of her. She sat on a high stool with Osas asleep on her back. We greeted her and the other women who sold meat and tomatoes close by.

My mother took her phone from Mirabel and placed it inside her wrapper. She took a long bench from one of the women who sold fish and asked us to sit down. After which she bought rice and stew tied in banana leaves so we could eat. Mirabel and I did not bother to use a spoon. We washed our hands with a sachet water and ate.

After eating, Mirabel chatted with one of the younger girls who sold palm nuts while I watched as people walked hurriedly around the market with strange looks on their faces. Everyone seemed to be annoyed by something. Maybe it was the flies that buzzed around the meat and fish or the fact that the place smelled because of the piling refuse in a corner. Some of the wheelbarrow pushers who helped people move their heavy goods shouted at the bus drivers to park their buses away from the road. A man selling rat poison and insecticides tried to sell my mother a pack of Rambo insecticide. She politely told him she did not need it. I was still engrossed in people watching when I heard my mom shout and drop her phone on the ground. I must have gone into shock because I became disoriented for a while. All I could see was my mom throwing her hands into the air and crying while other women came to her side. I could barely hear anything. I saw Mirabel join her. When I was able to hear clearly again I asked one of the women what had happened.

'Your papa don die,' she said to me. Your papa don die. Those words played over and over in my mind. I did not know what that meant for us other than we were not going to see my father ever again. I cried a lot thereafter. I cried till my body could no longer produce any tears.

Later on, I found out as my mother talked to sympathizers that my father had been in a motor accident. He had died instantly.

A lot of people came to our house to see how we were faring and a lot of them said the same words to me 'you're now man of the house. Take care of your mother and sisters.' I would nod my head in response.

After one month we were ready for the burial. It was not easy for my mother to get the money for it. She had to sell most of our things, part of which included our DVD player. It still had the power rangers' DVD plate inside. I resorted to holding the case which had pictures of the rangers on it as I slept. I would dream of them fighting and winning only to wake up to realize I could no longer watch them.

A few days after the burial ceremony as I walked back home after running an errand for my mother, I heard a familiar sound coming from Igho's house. The front door was opened. I peeked in to find Igho watching my Power Rangers with my DVD player. I did not think twice before shouting 'Ole!' and pounced on him. It took his elder brother all his strength to pull me from him. I walked back home with my pride deeply wounded. I knew my mother had sold the DVD player to someone I just did not know it had been to Igho's mother. For a brief moment I hated my father. I hated him for dying. If he had not died, the DVD player and Power Rangers would still be around.

The Writer

Erhu Amreyan is a Nigerian writer whose short stories have appeared in several literary magazines and anthologies. Her micro fiction 'Somewhere in Northern Nigeria' is currently running as a Google Ad.

She is a Ghibler who enjoys old classic rock songs and movies.

Mobile: +2347035050115

Email: erhuscarlet@gmail.com

Twitter: @erhuwrites

Instagram: @erhukome

In the end

by Phylix Chika

They say your life flashes before your eyes when you reach the end. Whoever came up with that... adage, probably hadn't fallen to his/her death before.

What flashed before my eyes wasn't my entire life. I couldn't even remember a good portion of what transpired in those early years. I did remember a sort of mid-life crisis, but that shouldn't be right. I wasn't past 40 years. What I vividly remembered was the gravest mistake I could ever possibly make.

Yakubu warned us. Yakubu warned us all. Pity... considering his was a rather pitiful death.

What is it with youthful exuberance? You believe that you can own the world and it should bow to your whims. We were young, wild — and as the song likes to point out — free. When we found something provocative, we liked to test it out. When we found something adventurous? That was our next journey. When we found keys that purported to open doors to the underworld, we scoffed and decided we were going to find the locks. Yakubu warned us though. He was the most spiritual member of our quaint group. The rest of us were a mixed bag of odds and ends. One has to wonder how we got along so well. I couldn't chalk it up to opposites attracting, because we were way off the opposite poles. It was a perfect fit, as much as perfect can be used in this world.

And we're all dead. Well, if you include me then we're all almost dead.

Do you believe in fate? What about destiny? Do you have this unassailable belief that whatever is meant to be will come to pass? Or are your beliefs just as abdicable as mine? I've never believed in fate. I've never believed that if you don't uphold your supposed destiny, then you've wasted your life. So... when we were told that we were to forfeit our lives after all is said and done, I think I actually snickered. Onyinye must have laughed hard when she saw the look on Yakubu's face after we were told of the end. Can't say I blame her... his face was oddly hilarious. What did we do to bring this upon us?

Simple really. We made a blood oath deal with a demon. And not just any demon... it (he?) had a name.

Amon.

Amon promised us riches untold for the low price of our souls, and we didn't even budge at the offer. What we wanted was something far more... idiotic. The best times of our lives. We found a summoning ritual, drew our blood on the seal, called upon a demon from the underworld and told it — him that all we wanted was to have the most exciting lives possible. We wanted the kind of vanity that would ring on even after we passed. I mean... records are broken, but at least the previous record owners are honoured one way or the other, right?

And exciting lives did we have. Our little group — Yakubu, Onyinye, Tunde, Sophia, Adeola, Fatima and myself — had the best lives anyone could possibly dream about. Dream jobs landed, dream locations visited, dream items bought... the level of materialism we reached was crazy. We couldn't always afford the biggest toys, but it seemed that our wishes didn't necessarily need the biggest toys to come to pass. Even better was how Tunde and Sophia finally tied the knot after the years of 'will-they-won't-they' we were all subjected to. Turns out, when the contract ended they were meant to off themselves.

Tunde and Sophia were the first to go. They were found with stab wounds all over their bodies, in their locked bedroom. Just one knife. The theory was that one stabbed the other and then stabbed him/herself. But how do you carry a knife and stab yourself ten times without remorse? How do you do that while you have a child sleeping not too far away in another room? Sophia was pregnant with another baby... we didn't even know

82

until the autopsy was done. Maybe they wanted to surprise us with the good news. If the cruellest possible outcome happens to the best of us, what then should the others expect?

Adeola's was a grotesque passing. At some point on a flyover, she lost control of her car and crashed on the side. The impact was hard enough to send her bursting through the windshield as her car careened on the edge. A broken-down signboard was below the crash point, and they say she spent the better part of 10 minutes screaming her lungs out as she was impaled on one of the signboard's beams. I can't even imagine how agonizing those last minutes could've been.

Fatima and I had a thing going on, though I think we both knew it couldn't lead to anything serious. That didn't stop us from exchanging house keys so we could 'drop by' should the need arise. On one of those 'dropping by' visits, I found her in the kitchen with her face submerged in a deep-fry pot. I can never get the smell of her burning flesh out of my mind. Reports say there were marks of a struggle, which means possibly someone had kept her head under as she thrashed around. I was lead suspect for a while, but I got dropped when there was no evidence pointing to me. That didn't make her death any less painful...

Before Fatima's death, Yakubu had been telling us how this was our doing. We had made an oath with Amon, and rather than honour our end of the deal and give up our souls, we continued to live on like we hadn't summoned a demon from the underworld. There's this thing about the human brain... it strives for rationality. Everything has to have an explanation. And if there's no plausible explanation? Then discard it and ignore that it exists. Intentionally ignore the fact that you may have actually tapped into the spiritual realm and chalk it up to someone who's playing a magic trick. And the change that has occurred after you wished for things to be more exciting? Call it the universe finally doing you a favour and seeing that you should be treated better than others. Either that, or you deserve the better treatment you're getting.

83

After Fatima's death, I think we all became open to the possibility that we were getting our dues because we didn't surrender our souls willingly. But how do you surrender your soul willingly? Kill yourself? That's what Yakubu thought... Yakubu was found in his blissful home, by his children, hanging by his neck off the top floor baluster of their lovely home's staircase. I don't even want to think about what it could've been like for the children to see their father dangling by his neck as foam and spittle drooled out of his hanging mouth.

Onyinye, bless her soul, was a fighter to the end. Always believed she could stand up to whatever bully was in your way. I wouldn't exactly have called Amon a bully, but I got her point. Her last stand was at a concert she was performing at. While she was on a solo number, one of the overhead lights fell on her. The angle was so spot on the glass broke and her head got stuck inside the fixture. Salt to injury was when the wires had her get a rather strong electric bath. It was quite a... shocking performance.

It belittles me to make a pun out of her demise, but I'm at the end of my rope. At this point, I say damn it all to hell, and to be sure that it is indeed damned to hell I've taken the liberty of being prepared. An overdose of painkillers taken with a few shots of tequila. And to top it all off, a nice dive from the top of a high-rise building. Probably excessive, but the idea is to die before I hit the ground, and to make sure that there's nothing left for me to bring back. Onyinye didn't die immediately... after all.

Life didn't flash before my eyes as I plunged to my death. Just the bits that led up to this moment. And, I'm not so sure, but I could've sworn I saw Amon looking down at me from the top of the building after I jumped. Doesn't really matter, does it? If after all this I still make it, maybe I'll write some kind of memoir that'll be laughed at for being too preposterous. A dead man can still dream, no?

The Writer

84

Armed with a gamepad in one hand and a keyboard in the other, Phylix's love of fiction and make believe is paralleled only by his love of creating fiction and make believe. And video games. He loves video games too.

Mobile: +2348028053415

Email: pcdonnay@gmail.com

Facebook: Phylix Chika

Jumoke's Cross

by Mobolaji Kafayat Olanrewaju

"What do you mean mum? Take it easy!"

My calm demeanor belied my racing heart, but my hands trembled as I spoke. Yinka noticed my agitation, grabbed my left hand and started rubbing it soothingly.

"Please, can you come over as soon as possible?" My mother replied. "I can't discuss this over the phone."

Her voice wavered at the end of the statement. Something was definitely wrong.

"Okay, mum. I'll be with you shortly. In the meantime, I want you to take things easy. Breathe. There's no point getting your blood pressure up unnecessarily. Please do that for me."

"I've heard you Olajumoke, but please pray hard. I don't want to lose you now. Don't delay, please."

With that plea, she broke off the connection.

***

"What is the problem, Jummy?" Yinka asked in a quiet voice. I'd forgotten he was still holding my hand, and his question yanked me back to my immediate surroundings.

"It's a family issue," I answered, getting to my feet. "I think I have to start going home now."

He stood up too and looked at my face searchingly.

"If you honestly believe I'll allow you to go alone in this state of mind, then you don't know me at all. Give me a second to grab my keys. I'll be with you shortly."

He disappeared into his bedroom and came back within a few seconds.

"I have to be at my mother's." I told him as we got into his car.

86

"I know. I heard you on the phone. Fortunately for you, I know the place; I was even there a few weeks ago. We'll be there in no time."

He grinned at me and turned the key in the ignition.

"It is not funny, Yinka. I already have enough on my plate without adding my sister's issue to the pile. What will my mother think if she sees both of us together? It will only buttress her opinion of me as a wayward person."

My tone sounded bitter to my own ears.

"If your mother actually has thoughts like that about you then I think she's not worthy of being your parent."

His statement was very emphatic. I turned away to look out of the window.

"What do you know anyway?" I mumbled under my breath. "How can you vouch for me when you've not even seen me in years? People change, you know?"

"Why not fill me in on the missing parts?" he begged tenderly. "You better get used to me being part of your life because as long as I know you still have feelings for me, I won't allow you to walk away."

The statement had a ring of finality to it. He engaged gears, switched on his blinkers, pulled out and joined the traffic.

***

Mother was in the sitting room when we arrived. Her face creased into a questioning frown immediately she spotted Yinka behind me.

"Good morning ma," he quickly greeted in anticipation of her query. "I know you're curious about why I'm here with Jumoke when you still saw me with Adenike a couple of weeks back. The thing is, Jumoke was mine before we got separated years ago. Somehow fate conspired to bring us back together that day Adenike brought me home."

His eyes had a solemn look as he spoke, and his voice echoed with sincerity. Mother paused for a few seconds when he finished, and then asked a question. She was looking at me as she did.

"How is Adenike taking it? Is she aware of this development?"

"Badly," I answered quietly. "Very badly. She caught us in a rather compromising position in his house the day she visited. I tried to explain to her on the phone afterward but she wouldn't listen. I'm sorry for hurting her, I didn't mean to."

A part of me was waiting for the expected tongue lash.

"But what were you doing in his house? I understand that you both have history, but since Adenike already got engaged to him, you should have just let things be. I don't think you should be involved with him again."

I clearly heard the accusation in her voice, and it triggered an ache at the base of my skull. Yinka came to my rescue.

"Ma, I broke up with Adenike before I went back to Jumoke. I'm not even sure if Jumoke is ready to take me back because she is more concerned about her relationship with her sister for now, but she's my other half and I will fight for her with my last breath."

There was a fire in his eyes as he paused and held my mother's gaze challengingly. I almost smiled when she backed down and looked away.

He pushed me forward.

"Go on Jummy. I believe there are more important issues to discuss for now, so I will excuse myself. I'll be waiting outside."

He squeezed my hand briefly and then turned to leave. I snatched at his.

"No please. I want you here with me. Stay, please."

88

He nodded. Together we walked to the twin-seater settee while mum watched. When we were comfortably seated I asked her about her trip.

"How was your trip to Ile-Ife?"

She also dropped into a seat opposite us and sighed heavily before she answered.

"The old man from that previous trip years ago is dead. I met his son who is also a Babalawo and explained everything to him. After consulting the oracle, he informed me that the goddess is angry. We were supposed to have brought you back to the shrine several times during your growing years for different sacrifices as we were instructed to do but we didn't. As our punishment for failing to follow instructions, she now wants you back. We have a seven-day ultimatum to deliver you to her shrine or there will be terrible repercussions."

Mother suddenly looked ten years older.

"Wait, first mum," I said. "In your desperation to have a child did you actually agree to that condition?"

She nodded grimly.

"Yes, my daughter. Yes, I did. Once you were born I didn't take it so seriously anymore, and later when it came to mind I went to church and prayed for deliverance."

"Well," I said, piercing the silence that had descended on the room. "I'm not ready to die yet, so you better start coming up with alternatives."

The furrows on her forehead deepened.

"The only alternative according to baba is to exchange your life with that of someone else, someone very dear to your heart. Of course, I volunteered myself, but the goddess refused. She wants someone closer."

"Someone closer? Like who? Adenike? Father? That reminds me. What about my father? Where is he? You've never given me a clear answer as to his whereabouts. All you've ever volunteered

89

is that he went on a trip and never came back. Where is he, mother? You started this thing together so you should sort it out the same way."

My voice rose several notches. At another time I would have stopped pestering her but this was not the time for sympathy. She looked completely distraught.

"Your father?"

I nodded, signaling her to continue.

"I caught your father on our matrimonial bed with another woman. When I asked him to make a choice between the two of us he picked her..."

I flew out of my seat in her direction but Yinka stopped me dead in my tracks with a cold command.

"Hold it right there, Jummy."

Mother stared with new respect at the man who just shut me up. I slumped back in my seat resignedly.

"Go on." I whispered. She did.

"My condition for granting him divorce was that he would never try to contact any of you and he agreed. I did what I thought was best for us all."

"You always know what is best for everyone." I sneered. Yinka gave me a reproachful look, then turned to address mother.

"I know this is a family issue that I'm not supposed to interfere in, but since I am here I'll just give you my own opinion. Whatever might have happened between you and your ex-husband is irrelevant at this point. Jumoke is still his daughter and he has every right to know what is going on, especially as this is a life and death situation."

"I know," mother answered in a subdued voice. "I'll try to reach him any way I can and hopefully we will find a solution in time. Already we have lost a day."

"I'm sure we will," Yinka stated reassuringly. I only nodded, wishing I was as confident as he sounded.

***

"Your father is here," Mother announced quietly, standing beside the half-opened door.

It was barely an hour since she made the promise to contact him. I jumped up from my seat, my mouth working furiously.

"What? Dad? How? Where?"

A man stepped into the room. I would have thought mother was lying, but he was actually here.

"Dad? Is that really you?" I asked in amazement.

"Yes, baby. It is, I'm here. Come!"

He held out his arms and I ran into them. Tears filled my eyes and spilled down my cheek as he hugged me tight and rocked me from side to side like he used to do when I was younger. Memories came flooding back.

"Why dad?" I wailed. "Why did you stay away for so long?"

"I'm sorry," he cooed. "Really, I am. It's complicated but you won't die I assure you. Your mother has updated me with the scenario on ground. You did nothing to deserve any of this, and I'll gladly replace your life with mine."

He cupped my cheeks affectionately.

"But I can't lose you, dad," I sobbed. "You just came back, I can't lose you again."

"Uncle Dewale? Is that you, Uncle Dewale?"

It was Yinka. He'd gotten to his feet and was staring at my dad in amazement. Dad let me go and moved towards him.

"Yinka! What in the world are you doing here?"

"It really is a small world indeed," Yinka said, shaking his head. "I didn't even know you had a family here in Lagos."

"Wait," I said, moving in between the two of them. "You know each other? How?"

Before any of them could answer, the closed door burst open again and Adenike rushed in. Her hair looked rough and her eyes were cold and scary. Something was weird about the way she ignored everyone else and stared at me expressionlessly.

A chill flew down my spine.

"Olajumoke Davies," she said in monotone. "You have overstayed your visit on this earth. It was written to be like this; that was why the ones that saw the end from the beginning asked me to come after you. Your fiancée has been waiting all these years and he is impatient for your return. Please go back to him and let me have my man. Yinka is mine."

A chilly wind swept through the room.

The Writer

Mobolaji Olanrewaju is a full time Travel consultant and a writer. She Loves reading and blogs at https://mobolajiolanrewaju.wordpress.com. She is a guest blogger at https://hogfurniture.com.ng. She can be reached on Facebook with the name, Olanrewaju Mobolaji or via her email, obolaji2002@yahoo.com. Her twitter handle is @obolaji.

Mobile: +2348124735845

Email: obolaji2002@yahoo.com

Facebook: Olanrewaju Mobolaji

Instagram: mobolaji.o

Twitter: @obolaji

Mercy

by Chisom Christabel Anyanwu

She twisted lazily on her bed, stretching her limbs and yawning loudly like a hungry dog. Her eyes

surveyed her surroundings and she concluded within her that she was alone. Her husband should already be at work so she could still steal some more sleep. She yanked the blanket over her head and was about to close her eyes when she felt something beside her. It was her husband's phone and she was almost about to lie on it. Her husband never went out without his phone so she was puzzled. Was he still at home? A part of her wanted to swipe the phone and look through but she instantly did otherwise. She kept the phone back on the bed with a frown, the last time she opened her husband's phone, she uncovered sordid details of his extra marital affairs. It was a long time since the incident but trusting her husband after it seemed to be more tedious than finding a job. What I don't know won't kill me, she muttered. The kitchen was alive with different sounds-clanking of pans, rushing of water and they all ushered in a very appetizing aroma. She snuggled under the blanket. She didn't need to check who it was in the kitchen, there were only two occupants of the house. She closed her eyes and pretended to be asleep when she heard his footsteps and whistling - she didn't want him to find her awake. Whatever reason he had for staying at home, hovering around in the kitchen, she wanted to find out. Jesse sauntered into the room carrying a tray, which contained a plate of fried rice and a small bowl of ice cream on it. He dropped the tray on the bedside table then hopped onto the bed. There was a small feather in his hand and he tickled his wife with it. "open your eyes sweetie." Lota pretended not to feel anything, she tried so hard not to burst into laughter when her husband tickled her. Jesse threw the feather aside, he knew the game she was playing. He kissed her lightly on

94

the cheek, then traced the circles of her ear with his tongue. She remained adamant, not even an eyelash moved. He kissed her on her eyes, then her beautiful lips curved into a smile. He smiled. His hard work was gradually paying off. "Baby, wake up. I made you breakfast." You only make breakfast when you have something to ask from me, she thought. Her lips creased from the smile which was already forming to a slight frown. The last time you made me breakfast, was the saddest day of my life. She had tried severally to erase the memory of the incident that caused an ugly dent in their marriage but she found herself reminiscing on it every time her husband tried to do something nice. She neither could forget nor forgive. *** His phone was ringing. She wanted to ignore it at first but the caller didn't seem to understand that the owner of the phone was busy. It was ringing continuously, disturbing her ear drums so she glanced at the screen and grabbed the phone. "Baby, did you get my text?" The high pitched female voice from the other end of the phone said, "my breast is dripping honey and I'm so wet and horny for you," she rattled on unaware of who picked up the call. "Who is this?" Lota yelled, a knot was beginning to tighten in her belly. She didn't want to believe that her husband kept a mistress. "I should be asking you that. What are you doing with my boyfriend's phone?" Obviously, somebody was mistaken. She must have dialed a wrong number. Lota had many thoughts running through her mind. "Your boyfriend?" She managed to ask calmly, hoping that her fears would soon be eased. "What are you doing with my boyfriend's phone, bitch? Where is Jesse?" The caller bellowed. She even called me a bitch. Tears ran down Lota's cheeks. "I am his wife." She said resignedly, the saliva in her mouth had gone sour already. She hung up on her husband's mistress and started sobbing. She hated her husband. She hated marriage. "I am a fool." She moaned. Her husband had a mistress who didn't even know he was married and she had been in the dark all the while. She stared at the empty plate of rice on the bedside table and her stomach rumbled, she wanted to throw up every single grain of rice she had eaten. Jesse had made her breakfast and even brought a bowl of oranges for her. Was this

95

how he made breakfast for his mistress? She thought of all the nice things he had always done for her and she choked knowing he might have done more for the lady. After all it is said that men spend more on their mistresses. She pulled her bowl of oranges from the bedside table, balanced it on her laps and began to peel an orange, slowly, thinking about how to let her husband know that she had found out his secret. All the instructions from the marriage class they both attended began to play in her head. "Respect him. Feed him and give him sex and he'll never leave you. Be a good wife and a good mother and you'll keep your man forever." They only taught them how to keep a husband, but nobody discussed about how to punish him. Jesse came out of the bathroom, humming a song. His sparkling white towel was wrapped around his waist and few drops of water clung to his hairy legs making him look like a model who advertised towels. He paced towards his wife who sat on the bed peeling oranges with her back facing him. Her black hair tumbled down to her perfectly curved waist and her legs were crossed-yoga fashion. He knew he was supposed to start dressing for work but he didn't, instead he cupped her breasts from behind, baring his teeth and smiling sheepishly. He smelt fresh. He licked the nape of her neck and gave her nipples a tender squeeze. She gasped and tried to push him away but he held her tight. He turned her towards him and kissed her, caressing her body as he lowered himself on her. He let his fingers slide along her thighs while he sucked gently on her nipples. "Get of me! Leave me alone!" She shoved him away and shifted to the edge of the bed. "Baby, what is it?" He closed in on her, tugging gently at her hair and tenderly kissing her chin. She burst into tears. "Go away. Go to her." She realized that she was ignorant of the lady's name. "You're cheating on me!" she blurted out in rage, "she called. Your mistress." Jesse stood up abruptly, looked around for his phone, when he found it, he checked the call log and hissed. "I'm sorry honey. It's not what you think." He drew closer to his wife, puckered his lips and was about to give her a peck when she slapped him. "Get away from me, your filthy dog!" You've been deceiving me. How many years have you known her? I guess you

96

didn't even wait for our marriage to be consummated before you brought your hoe into the picture." "Baby, please. Let me explain. She..." He stuttered and fidgeted trying to touch his wife who was already wailing. "Just shut up. How long? Tell me, what does she do for you that I can't?" She began to hit him, "your horny bastard." "I'm sorry baby. Please forgive me. I'll end everything now. I will. I promise. Just listen to me first." He pleaded. "Forgive you? Never!" She moved towards the edge of the bed grabbed her bowl of oranges, on a second thought, she dropped it back. She grabbed the knife inside the bowl and turned towards her husband, "you'll never cheat on me again." He leapt from the bed on seeing her with the knife, and tried to disarm her but his towel loosened and fell off. She took advantage of that and kicked him in the groin. He yelled for mercy but she paid no heed. She stabbed his chest, and his belly. Fiercely poking the knife into his body as if she were digging a well. Blood oozed freely from the cuts and she kept yelling, "you'll never cheat on me again!" she grabbed his limp penis and hacked it off in an instant, "never!" As she held the lump of flesh in her hand, she broke down in tears. *** "Baby, why are you crying? Wake up. I made breakfast." Lota opened her eyes. She didn't mean to sleep at all, it was supposed to be a prank. A wave of pity enveloped her as she saw him bending over her, she wiped her face clean with her hands and hugged him. "Promise you'll never make me sad again."

The Writer

97

Chisom Christabel, otherwise known as Krystalz, is a student of The University of Portharcourt. Writing has been one of her many passions since childhood. Apart from writing, she likes acting and singing.

Mobile: +234**7062095116**

Email: chisomchristabel5@gmail.com

Facebook: Chisom Christabel

The Runaway

by Olutosin Olubunmi Ajanaku

I like the way Jerry says my name without really seeing me there. He drawls it out like a silent prayer, like a whisper to a god you know has already answered your prayers, a sigh.

"Nesi"

"Yes brother"

"Get me a cup of Akamu"

"Yes brother"

"Nesi, take this dirty cup away"

"Yes brother"

He knows I'm always there and he never needs to yell or look around for me. You know he is at peace. The way he sits still, bent over his books. Even when Jerry speaks, his body is still. If not for the slim lemon grass that dangles loosely from his lips that gives him away, you would think he is a statue. He is always chewing lemongrass. He says it helps him think. Maybe lemon grass has a thinking spirit, but I am yet to find it. I have tried once or twice, to think and chew. Maybe the fault is mine, and I have no thoughts, or it is one of those things you acquire when you become learned like Jerry, I don't know. As for me, I have decided I prefer my lemon grass when it is soaked in hot water and cooked with black tea.

I like it when Jerry studies. His brows are furrowed, like he is having a deep conversation with the village Chief. I wish I could do that, but when I flip through the browning leaves, all I see is tiny shapes, printed in ink. Even Jerry's notebooks make less meaning than those prints. You would think cockerels soaked their feet in ink, and had a party on the pages of his notebooks. The edges of his books flop over like the ears of our house dog, from over use. The new ones are sharp at the edges, but only remain so for a very short time. I'm always stationed by his reading post, inspecting all his books with a protective eye, and I always take note of these little differences. I keep hoping some of the knowledge in his books would pour on me just by being so close to them, but nothing has happened yet. Even when he is gone; I remain firmly rooted at the foot of his reading table. There should be a rank for persons like me who sit by reading posts all day. When he leaves for mission school, he doesn't need to take his books out of the verandah. He knows I will keep an eye on them till he returns. He knows for certain that I won't wander off. I have always begged him, to teach me what those shapes mean, or show me what my name would look like, but he refuses.

I don't go to mission school. My father says girls aren't meant to go to school. We are made to learn cooking, home keeping and child bearing. It is our duty to care for our men and children. Sometimes, I wonder, if I were a boy, if I went to school, what it would be like.

Maybe I would wear white dresses with the funny hats the nurses in the mission hospital wear. Papa says nurses are prostitutes who will never find good husbands, but whenever we fall ill, mama and papa take us to the hospital, and speak to the nurses with respect. I don't think it is okay that they expose us to prostitutes.

Sometimes, I pass by them in the village and I make sure to walk on the other side of the road. Yet, I secretly envy their clothing, and wonder if there are other ways I could go to school and dress like that and still make a good wife.

I like the way Jerry dresses too. He wears starch stiffed cotton shirts and tucks them inside Khaki trousers. He holds it together with cow hide belt father insists is Italian leather, but I know it isn't.

Every morning, I fire up the coals, and fill up the iron. When the shiny plate has become hot, I call on Jerry. He spends hours bent over his shirt every day, ironing out the creases, till the shirts are so fine, the edges threaten to cut you. Jerry says Father Francis says a dignified man takes care of his looks. When he is done, he gives me the iron to empty out the hot coals, and douse the heat but when no one is watching, I try to imitate him, and iron over the frayed edges of my skirts. But the iron is usually too hot and it burns me. I make a mental note to take the skirts off before ironing, but I always forget. I only remember after I've been burned.

Jerry is the only one who goes by his English name in our household. Jerry's native name is Ekenedilichukwu, but when he was applying to go into mission school, his name was too long, and wouldn't fit into the boxes provided in the forms, so father told them to write his baptismal name Jeremiah. Father says a name bonds a man with his people. If Jerry bears his baptismal name, he will be closer to his teachers because they would understand. One day, he came home and told us to call him Jerry, so we did. No questions asked.

My name is Nesiama, and I have never told anybody to call me Margaret. The only place you will see Margaret is in my birth certificate and Obituary after I am over hundred and dead, because all my teeth have fallen.

I am only 9 years old, and hundred is a long time from now. I like Nesi, pending that time.

One day, a long time ago, Jerry forgot his lunch box, and mother made me take it to his school. It was the first day I would be visiting the school. It was a massive building at our village entrance. The classrooms are full of boys in white and grey Khakis like Jerry's, with only a sprinkle of girls wearing pinafore. I shook my head in bewilderment. Only an uncaring parent would send a girl child to brave the dangers of school knowing fully well what they could become. But then, the nurses in the hospital today would grow old, and then we would need new people to give us our medicines.

I couldn't find Jerry in his classroom, so I asked to see the matron who we all called "Mother superior" in church. Mama asked me to greet her, and also give her a basket of ripe Ube.

"Down the hall, see that office in front? That is her office." The students directed me.

I entered Mother Superior's office, and say Jerry's head pop up from under her skirt. I walked in and greeted them both respectfully, but they didn't seem too pleased to see me. I dropped the Ube on her table, and Jerry walked me out of the office immediately.

Jerry seemed relieved to be out of Mother Superior's office. I wonder why he was in her office while his classmates were in the classroom. He took his lunchbox from me without a word.

He turned around and made for class then paused.

"I was only helping matron pick up her ink pen that fell"

I stared at him, and nodded my head vigorously. I didn't understand why he felt the need to explain.

"No word of this to anybody at home. Okay?"

"Okay"

"Who is watching my books?'

Scared I had done a grave sin, I rushed all the way home, without stopping to catch my breath. I forgot to tell him his shirt tail was hanging out, but it didn't matter.

Jerry was different to me ever since. He would lecture me about being your brother's keeper. He even taught me how to draw my name in English alphabets. He watches me closely, and keeps me close to him. Every morning before leaving home, he would ask me if I told anybody anything, and I would shake my head.

Jerry returned from school one day, fuming with anger. I was waiting eagerly to show him that I wrote my name, but he was not interested. He looked me in the face and I saw his eyes were filmy, and glistening as if he was about to cry. That scares me. I always did my best to remain invisible. Invisible children get to eat twice a day, and don't get lashing tongues of horse whips licking their backs.

102

"Did the post man come today?" He asked intently. There's a pregnant bead of sweat resting on his eyelash, threatening to fall. If he blinks, it might drop in his eye, and the saltiness would sting him there. I was watching anxiously, I forgot to answer.

His huge hands landed across my face, and my palms jerked up, rubbing the sting vigorously, before the welts of palm prints formed on my face.

The answers came flooding

"Yes. Posumanu con hia" I blurted out in my heavily accented grammar. Even in the face of fear, no child of Mr. Dan forgets his grammar.

"Which letter did you give to him?!"

"I gi am lettah wey dey top table" I answered. Jerry had only one assignment for me today. When the post man comes, give him the very important letter on the study table.

The postman came is his shiny bicycle, carrying a leather bag by his side. He asked if we had a parcel, and I said yes. Jerry showed me the letter and told me clearly "This letter is very important. It will take me to the missions' headquarters in Lagos for a scholarship test. If I pass, I will go to the university. Do you understand?"

I nodded fervently, rejoicing that Jerry has made it in life. When he buys his new house, he will send for me. I dared not miss the postman.

I watched intently as Jerry licked the stamp, and stuck it on the white envelope.

I was happy he trusted me with something so important. The postman came at 11:00am and asked for Jerry's package.

The envelope he showed me was neatly placed inside his big leather book he writes in every night. That brown book was very precious to Jerry. He would never let even a fly land on it.

"Is that all? The post man asked, flipping the envelope back and forth, making faces like it looked too flimsy.

"Yessa"

"Are you sure?" He queried, and I thought for a second. If the postman thinks this letter is too small, does this mean Jerry would fail to impress them in the school? He spends his time studying and writing. I also found the envelope too flimsy, so I added the big brown book.

"This one too." I said, and the postman smiled

"Why did you forget to add that one?"

He packaged the big book and Jerry's letter in a bigger envelope and sealed it. I stayed with him to make sure everything was secure.

Why I have now earned this slap, I do not know.

One day, a group of people came to look for Jerry. Papa looked up at them. They were dignitaries in well ironed French suits. Papa's eyes were red, as they had been since the day Jerry left.

"My son has run away. I don't know why. I tried my best, I gave him all I have" Papa's voice trailed off and he dropped his head. I watched his shoulders shake violently as they whispered some news to him. I heard something about a dreadful woman being fired. I also heard them saying they would be happy to help find Jerry. Papa sobbed silently through the meeting, as he has done many times when he thinks no one is watching.

I remain settled in my corner, where the books are collecting dust; invisible and eagerly waiting for someone to call me.

The Writer

Olutosin lives in the quiet parts of Ogun State Nigeria with her family. She is a pastry chef, Quantity Surveyor, and an interiors designs consultant. She also volunteers for the Mentally Aware Nigeria Initiative She has a passion for telling African stories and taking them to the world.

Mobile: +2347068058106

Email: oolutosin14@gmail.com

Facebook: Olutossen Ajanaku

Instagram: @teechudley

Twitter: @teechudley

One Last Thing

by Jordan Oziegbe Eguavoen

Almost over. It was almost over, the dust, the incessant wailings and the drunken dancers. In their faded black coats, black hats and dust covered shoes they weren't exactly drunk, only their jerky and seemingly confused movements were. The four of them, with the coffin on their shoulders, moved forward, sideways like they would trip and fall, backwards and turned completely round before progressing forward again. It felt wrong that they were dancing to the jazzy tune of trumpets while his mother and siblings followed behind morosely. People he had never seen, like that fat woman with green veins on her laps that peeped from beneath her skirt, were the ones weeping. He heard someone say his uncle paid them to do that.

It all felt stupid and he wished its end passionately. Earlier at home, when they had opened the coffin for all to see his lifeless body as it lay as if asleep and Pastor had been talking to everyone present about life and death, he had tried to leave. The limitations of the physical eyes had been torn when the Sienna had lifted him from the roadside and into the gutter where he cracked his head on the edge. Certain things were revealed. He knew the married pastor had proposed a fling to his mother about a year after his father's death and that she had refused. He knew his mother allowed them to continue worshipping in the church because it was the only branch in their area and she didn't know how to explain why she wanted to stop. He and his siblings were extremist inquisitors and they knew her too well. He also knew that Pastor had succeeded with his little sister of fifteen years. He tried to leave but could not. He couldn't get more than ten steps from his body and couldn't influence anything in the physical either. But it was almost over now. His siblings had dropped dirt on his coffin and once his mother did too, he would be free. Free to leave, to see his father again, but also free for one last thing.

106

She stared at the dirt in her palm until her eyes watered. Her frame shook lightly, then violently until she broke. She knelt and crept towards the gaping hole his body had been lowered into.

"My boy, my son," she cried deeply. The late afternoon sun had caused her to be drenched in sweat and her hair was messy. She had not let anyone help her with it. "Why na, ehn? Do you hate me? What did I do to you? Why did you leave me?"

He wasn't sad, only furious. And the more she spoke the angrier he got. He was mad at the pastor who was taking advantage of his family and at life that wouldn't let up. His mother wept until all the strength left her, then Dave, his elder brother, came close and lifted her. She dropped the sand with a glaze and left.

At first it was a vibration, then freedom. Absolute freedom. Pastor was still there with his aged bible in both hands. He was talking to his sister. His only sister. He ran and dove through him.

***

It would start with inexplicable weakness and vomiting. Doctors would reassure him repeatedly that it wasn't anything serious. They would prescribe drugs to no effect, then he would visit herbalist homes in search of relief. By the time it manifested as full-blown cancer, it would be too late for Pastor.

The Writer

107

Jordan is a poetry and prose enthusiast. He is twenty two years old and a student of mathematics at the Ambrose Alli University, Ekpoma.

Mobile: +2348124735845

Email: Testimonies2016@gmail.com

Facebook: Jordan Eguavoen(Oz)

Instagram: @J_the writer

Road to yesterday

by Lota Dibua

The security officer had first found her in front of the office's gate crumpled on the floor like a folded duvet.

Later that day, I didn't know what attracted her to me, thus making me interested in their chitchat.

"So how old are you?" Lady Anna asked.

"Fourteen," She replied timidly.

Maybe it was because she had same features as I did, when I was fourteen; too tiny for her age, eyes shining brightly and trying otiosely to hide those fears, the uncertainties too. Mouth that wants to wail and cry out the pains, hankering for freedom, but just can't. Maybe it's because of the scar lying smoothly on the black patch above her left eyelid; like a beautiful work of art. I have mine too, a big black patch trailing from my forehead to my left cheek; the devils mark, it was termed, not until now.

"Wow! You don't look it. You look ten." Lady Anna replied.

I noticed it this time, her facial reaction after this comment; angered, dumbfounded, uncertain, excitement, frightened. I noticed it all...

It got creepy, I suddenly developed goose bumps despite the heat from the scorching sun, no thanks to global warming and the office canteen that had no shade.

Did she get the scar from a smelly, tatterdemalion prophet that cared more about the whips than his old rugged life and money? Had the prophet confirmed her a witch?

***

November, 1997.

"Chukwu naru ekwensu ike." The prophet would exclaim whilst his whip danced merrily all over my body. Those cattle reared by the Fulani herdsmen had nothing on me. And like the carcass of an antelope, I'd lie later, tied to the guava tree in the open compound, the one that bore similarities to the fig tree cursed by Jesus, just leafless...

When the moon is shining in the sky, and the guava tree casts a shadow on the open compound; as part of my cleansing exercise, the same prophet would insert his fingers into my private parts. So deep would his fingers go, as though hunting for a gold mine.

***

Had her mother adhere to the prophet's idea of incarceration and starvation?

"My Mama wan kill me." Her response to lady Anna's question as regards to the whereabout of her parents startled me.

"Because I be winch." She continued pointing at the black patch on her forehead.

***

March, 1998

"You see dis my pikin, Ije, na winch she be." My mother was ever ready to provide this answer to anyone who questioned her concerning her actions. And she was believed, after all I had the devil's mark- the black patch.

I could be likened to the rods that served as burglarproof to the small window of my confinement: thin, red and rusted, rusted from the scars of the prophet's whip.

***

Will she stab her dad when she turns 11? Will she get tired of his sexual molestations?

***

August, 1998.

110

He would come again, to my confinement- the small, one windowed room. He would pick me up and carry me to the parlour; throwing me roughly on the cough, I would watch his big frame penetrate the insides of me. I knew better than offer any form of resistance; better than letting him bombard me with those slaps, and the terrible kicks on my tummy. He'd have his way after all.

I crawled, after Papa was done, to the kitchen beholding the glorious beauty of the kitchen knife.

"Just a thrust and all this would be over," A voice said to me.

But the voice was wrong. Three thrusts, and the man called Papa was rendered helpless.

Three thrusts, more stabs and I left him looking like the vegetables, ending this age long abomination.

I came to the realization of my action when I heard the cry of mama on her return to meet the body of her husband.

Run. Just what I did. I ran to the open hands of my freedom.

I ran to corper Rita; the one who taught social studies in the community school and headed the club - I'm a girl child. Through her, I had my liberation. Through her, my lifelong dream was brought to fruition. Through her, I was saved from "the devils mark". I met the Save The Children Foundation through her. I was untagged a witch, I got a second chance to live, more like a human this time.

***

Oh! She' fourteen already. Could all this have happened? Is her liberation near?

"So Ijeawele, your mama wan kill you because you be witch?" Lady Anna asked fighting back the tears that threatened to blind her...

111

Her name is Ije. She's fourteen. Could she be the road to my yesterday?

Translation:

Chukwu naru ekwensu like - God take power from the devil.

The Writer

Lota Dibua. Lover of the pen experience. An engineering student also.

Mobile: +2348168587969

Email: lotadibua9@gmail.com

Facebook: Lota Dibua.

112

Seeing The Day

by Ekomobong Monday Ekpenyong

I was more or less a living zombie, having been born blind and dumb. The only thing which differentiated me from a zombie was because I could hear. My whole life was filled with trips to the hospital for drugs and medication. I totally depended on others to live. Mama often told me that I am a special child with unique abilities. I found nothing special in myself except the absurd pity and coaxed love which I was showered with. Mama understood the basic sign language but it wasn't enough

to feel the communication void in me. I longed for someone to talk with in my own way, someone who lives in the same world like me.

I always wondered how the trees looked like when it swayed; how the sky looks when it rained; how the sun seemed like with its dazzling hot

rays, which felt like a whiff of hot smoke from an oven; how the flowers looked, how its buds opened every morning. I always drowned in my imagination and my vague illusions of reality. Each new day met me with a gloom despite how bright Mama wowed it to be. Three months to my birthday, mama brought a maid to assist her in taking care of me while she was away on her busy schedules. Vera was the maid Mama brought for me, she was from Equatorial Guinea. When I met her, I ran my hands on her body to feel her height. She was tall like the pillar that stood on our balcony, her fingers were rough at the tips and she had a salty scent around her that I could almost taste it.

On the day Vera I realized that there was more to seeing than looking. I began to feel colours, taste them and separate them from each other. Vera had a pitched voice which sounded like the wrens that lived on our almond tree, each time she walked; she carried with her the scent of nutmeg and lavender; her smiles

113

were like April rains-small drops of breath that gave birth to large platters of pearly laughter. It always rung the tiny scorpions that stung my black heart and threatened to calm the throbbing pain I felt each time someone laughed or spoke.

Vera would hold my hands each time and teach me more difficult sign language. She would sing in her Spanish accent and bade me to see her dance.

"This girl doesn't have a heart." I heard Vera say one morning to mama. Mama lashed back at Vera and told her to not make life more complicated for my already difficult life.

"You're making her life more miserable" Vera lashed back. Her voice rung with suppressed tears that threatened to burst out like an inflated balloon.

"Do what your only paid to do and don't get too emotional with my daughter".

I heard Vera give out short hurting sobs as she slammed the door after mama had left. Everyday mama bought me electronic gadgets and machines, which she thought would make life more comfortable for me. I was not allowed to leave the house. If ever I did, I was only driven round town in air-conditioned infested cars that stank of toxic songs with phony American accents. I never saw the zooming cars, never felt them but I heard the blaring of horns-the noisy life that came with living in towns. I longed to feel the drop of fresh air, the salty stench of the sea air, the rush of crystal water and the ruffle of grasses as the wind caressed

it.

On my birthday Vera had promised to take me out to the park. I knew what being in the park was like; noisy children yelling for mummies, giggling teenagers rambling about latest dates, blares from rusty sounding

microphones, that made me think of Armageddon. I couldn't see them. I only heard them but I could feel them like the wind.

114

Hearing without seeing tasted like thick brown coffee that had no flavor or sweetness, it was only just bland and you could neither spit it out for its sourness nor swallow it for its sweetness.

My birthday came with storms and black cumulus clouds which Vera said looked like a naked black maiden in an uncombed afro. Vera's descriptions of my environment never hurt me. She said it with sincerity and with a bonding that wasn't masked with pity or coaxed love. She told me I could see but in a unique and more in-depth way which others could not. I began at last to see my blindness as a gift from Pandora's

box and the one distinct thing that stood me out from the rest.

It was windy and wet when Vera took me out. We rode in a rickshaw. I felt the slow motion of the breeze as it caressed my starved skin. I felt the little droplets of rain water as it landed on my hair and clothes. I heard clearly the noisy blares of car horns, speakers, megaphones, yells of traders and vulgar remarks from enraged drivers. I was beginning to see the day. Vera was quiet all through the ride to her mystery location and only spoke out when she held my hands and spelt "L.O.V.E" in it. I felt her smile back when I held her hands and spelt it back.

The mystery location was strangely quiet when we arrived that I suddenly became nervous. I motioned for Vera to be sure of her presence but she was quiet. I began to grope about as my heart thumped in fright.

Hot beads of sweat had begun to form on my forehead.

"Find me dear. It is hide and seek. Don't fret I am here with you".

Vera called out from a distance. I smiled widely, my first real smiles in years as I nodded excitedly. I groped my hands about the place and I felt the rough scrape from a shrub bush. I traced my steps gingerly and heard the rustling of dry leaves, trees whizzed in reply to the wind's call; it sounded like the F sharp on my keyboard; soft and melodious bearing the raspy voice of Celine Dion when she sang "The power of Love".

I felt a soft flutter in my heart and gave a hoot. I was with Mother Nature; I was basking in her euphoria and splendor. Soon I heard the loud splatters of water around me. It came with a force so strong that I lifted up the hem of my embroidered skirt. The force brought it down with such magnitude that caused it to fold around its base. The vacuum in my soul had begun to fill and what I had sought for many years had found me like a rising in the sun.

Seething flames of anger at Mama engulfed me but it was met with a reluctant ice of peace which extinguished it. Mama had denied me the need to see nature for all the years I had lived. She let me drown in pools of bitterness and oceans of pain that reminded me of living life the way I had come to find it. I stood there holding my head in pride as I savoured the environment. I felt like a lioness lying in the safari and for a moment I wanted to cry; I wanted to cry at man's stupidity in changing the environment from what it was to an abode that stank with blood, violence and harmful terrestrial habits. An earth that bore patiently the pangs of cruelty like a laboring woman holding her waist in suppressed pain as she brought forth a new life. Nature did that but we failed to see it. She has died multiple times so that man and all that is in it could survive.

"Dear." Vera called softly from somewhere behind me. "You didn't find me."

I held her hands and spelt the words "N, A, T, U, R, E I, S B, E, A, U, T, I, F, U, L" Into it.

Vera laughed that laughter that calmed the stinging scorpions in my heart

and made me want to cry.

"Cry sweetie, it is good for the soul". She said as she held my head into her bosom and stroked me fondly. I did cry. Letting it out in bits until it became one loud burst of spurting fountains.

"Come follow me Senorita. I will take you to a place where you will

116

badland, mon amigo."

She tucked at my hands after wiping my tears with my hair and I followed her trail.

We were at the shore. The air smelt of salt and the sand were fine soft grains that slipped from my fingers when I held it. Vera led me into the water and we stood knee deep in it. My eyes went watery and my tell-tale heart threatened to burst from joy as I heard the sound of the sea waves, rising and falling with the tide. I had finally begun to see the day in the way I had long sought for. The day began with the rising of the sun

from the horizons, somewhere in between the sky and the sea. The day began with flowers opening their buds and people letting out rolls of whispers. The day began with the sea pulling back its embrace from the sandy shore. The day began with water falling from a high hill, spurting tufts of strong air and splashes of pearly water. The day began with trees swaying in joy from the return of the sun and dripping with droplets of the morning due.

And later I would hear the voice of Vera in one of our trips to the beach saying. "And without a drop of water and a breath of fresh air the world will be in gloom and purgatory."

Beneath me is the cold sea water and wily waves that I can almost touch it. I am Angie Water and I am still, glittery, pearly and rushing like the waters of the ocean. I had finally begun to see the day for the first time in 16 years. The day is like blue waters in a white bottle.

The Writer

Ekomobong Ekpenyong is my name. I am 18 years. I am female. I live in Nigeria and study Communication Arts in the University of Uyo, Nigeria. I love writing, travelling, and lying on my messy bed while thinking of the crazy way the world spins. When I am not writing, I am grooming my Afro.

Mobile: +2347013843094

Email: ekommnd@gmail.com

Facebook: Adiaha Ekomobong

Instagram: eky mondy

The Big Four

by Charles Kadib

Saturday: Market Junction, Mgbogoba

12:30pm

Ola frowned when the jeep parked in front of his vulcanizing shade. From the look of the tire he could see that the work would take a while. The owner jumped down from the car and moved hurriedly towards Ola, even though the distance between the road and the shade was a small one. The man was a short stocky man, dressed in a white jumper. Though he didn't try to show it but he pulsated with nervous energy. He asked about if Ola was the vulcanizer and Ola replied in the affirmative. The man quickly told him what was wrong. In his mind, it was a straightforward process; fix the tire, pay the money and get where he was going as soon as possible. However, Ola sighed and looked longingly across the bar where fans were beginning to arrive for the Chelsea game. He shook his head and informed the man that he couldn't do the job that day. Amazed, the man asked why not. Ola couldn't reply but still insisted he just couldn't.

"But I'm in a hurry. I want you to do it fast."

"Then make I direct you go my friend for down the road."

"I have already been there, I didn't see anyone." The man said impatiently.

Ola nodded again. He should have known that Yusuf would not miss today's game. The match was pivotal; should Chelsea win today, they would climb to the top of the league. Last season when Manchester United had won, Yusuf who was a Man U fan had thrown jabs at Ola for two months. He thought about it now and his heart hardened, now it was his turn and he wasn't going to miss it for anything. The jeep owner was still insisting, even

119

offering to pay as high as ten thousand naira but Ola still shook his head.

"My instruments no dey here." He lied, "If you fit wait."

"I can't wait." Said the owner.

The man drove his car slowly away because of the bad wheel. Ola rushed towards the bar where the game was already twenty minutes in. He saw Yusuf at a corner with a bottle in front of him. He smiled at Ola and beckoned to him. As he sat down he glanced at the Screen and saw that the game was still goalless.

"Dem dey pepper una." Yusuf said.

Ola bought a beer and paid for the one being drunk by Yusuf. A man close to him lit a cigarette and the standing fan blew the choking fumes directly into Ola's lungs. He coughed and glared at the man who was absentmindedly talking with his friend. On cue, the friend of the man also lit his own cigarette. Then they scored against Chelsea. Yusuf celebrated with great zeal; Ola was bitterly criticizing the coach.

"Nonsense man." He shouted repeatedly.

As the game neared its end, Ola grew more desperate. He voiced out that Chelsea owed him a winning after all he had sacrificed to watch the game. Yusuf asked him what he had sacrificed and Ola told him.

"Fool." Pointed out Yusuf.

Chelsea lost the game and Ola angrily packed up for the day, then he went home to see if he would find an excuse to beat his wife.

Saturday: Alakahia, Choba

04:30pm

Although Moses was supposed to meet his friends so that they could complete the assignment that was due on Monday; he made an impulsive decision. He would stop at the viewing center at the junction of his street. He always loved that center. Unlike the others which were always cramped with people and extremely

120

hot; this one was aerated by four strategically placed fans. The seats were comfortable, they had three LED TVs so you could watch simultaneous games, and they had chilled drinks to occupy you as you watched. All these meant that you paid double what was paid in other centers but Moses didn't mind.

The game was just starting as he sat down. His club Manchester United were playing, dressed in their red and black. Half of the inhabitants of the bar were United fans although there were a few Chelsea and Arsenal fans also seated. It was easy to dictate the Chelsea fans by the scowl on their faces; Now it was Manchester United who would climb to the top of the league since Chelsea had lost. By his side, a Blues fan was drinking beer and insulting the Manchester coach and players. His comments quickly got on Moses' nerves who asked him to keep quiet.

"You think say we be Chelsea?" he asked sarcastically.

Some minutes later, Manchester United scored and Moses gave the Chelsea fan a knowing look but the man was not impressed. He said that the other team would equalise, he said it so nastily that Moses called him a fool who didn't know how to watch games.

"Anybody with an eye knows Man U will win this game."

The man told him to put his money where his mouth was. They both agreed to bet four thousand each, a neutral person, an obvious Arsenal fan was asked to hold the money. Moses briefly wondered what he would tell the other members of his assignment group if he lost the money. They would have no way of paying the Lab for the Chemical analysis which was pivotal to their assignment. He shrugged off the feeling immediately, his club would not lose and as if to agree with him, Manchester scored again. Fifteen minutes later another goal put Man United three goals ahead. It was now obvious that they would win. Moses was so ecstatic that he pulled off his shirt and danced provocatively in front of the Chelsea fan. The man shoved him aside roughly, Moses lost his balance and crashed against the wall. On getting up, he realized that he had cut a side of his face badly.

121

The sight of his own blood caused him to snap and without thinking, he took a beer bottle from one of the tables and smashed it on the man's head. A friend of the Chelsea fan retaliated and a huge brawl ensued which ended up with Moses severely battered.

It was only when his arm was being bandaged by a nurse in a nearby 'chemist' shop that he realized he had not collected the money he bet on the game.

Sunday: Rumuokwachi, Ozuoba

12:30 pm

One of the challenges of being an Arsenal fan in a place like this was the difficulty in seeing where to watch Arsenal games. The only time it got easy was when they played against Chelsea and Manchester United. Victor rode his bike persistently across the town, darting from bar after bar and drawing blank. There wasn't even a viewing center in the area.

As he gave up and started pedaling home, he spotted a crowd of people gathered at the door of a Barbershop. The barber was a light skinned man with elongated lips which looked like he had been sucking on lollipops for years. He was angrily driving away the hangers on. He needed only those who came for a haircut. Victor quickly signed up for one. The barber's mouth swung open; if they cut Victor's hair any lower than it was already the man would be bald. But the barber shrugged and admitted Victor in because business was business and who was he to complain. It would however, turn out to be one of the most frustrating haircuts he had ever tried to give as Victor kept turning and jerking ever so frequently. Finally, the frustrated barber promised Victor that he could stay and watch the game to the end if he promised to sit still. Victor managed to sit still but a near miss from an Arsenal player caused Victor to leap out of the chair. The clipper of the barber went at an odd tangent, carving a ridiculous line across his head.

"Na wa o." Sighed the man, "We go get to skin everything."

122

Victor did not care because at that time, Arsenal had scored and he was in a jubilant mood. While the barber removed every vestige of hair from his head, he talked about the brilliant history of Arsenal.

"Pepper them, Sanchez, pepper them!" he said in reaction to the displays of one of the Arsenal players.

Trouble however started when the game was over and he looked at his face in the mirror. A red line was still visible on his bare head and it was now throbbing painfully. He looked like someone who had just come out of a cancer operation. He tapped the red mark tenderly before glaring at the bewildered barber. He agreed to pay the fee only after an Almighty quarrel. But he was so distressed with how he looked and by the throb in his head that he did not see a rock lodged awkwardly in his path.

Onlookers would later recount, with varying degrees of exaggeration, how a cyclist had struck a stone and tumbled face first into an open overflowing ditch.

Sunday: Rumualogue, Ozuoba

04:30 pm

On a normal day, Uche's problem would have been over. His club Arsenal had won earlier in the day, his family had eaten lunch and gone to sleep, and there was enough fuel in the generator to watch the Liverpool game. He was however still uneasy. He brought out the betting slip from his pocket and glanced through it again. He had used his Child's school fees to bet on the games because his friend had assured him the games were sure bets. He trusted Chidi when it came to betting games. For two months straight, he had watched as Chidi steadily raked in five thousand every weekend. The guy was meticulous about his games and was uncannily accurate. When his mother in law had died and he was asked to raise a hundred thousand as his share of the burial expenses he turned to Chidi.

"Do you have any bulk money?"

"My children's school fees. About thirty thousand."

123

"Good."

Chidi then took him to a nearby betting center and picked out games for him. The Liverpool game was the last and Chidi had warned him he was unsure of that game. Just play it win or draw, he advised his friend, I know Liverpool won't lose but I'm not sure they would win. But calculating the odds later, Uche found that the money accrued would not cover his children's fees and the burial. However, playing Liverpool direct winning would tip it in his favour and give him extra beer money.

"Don't be greedy." Advised Chidi, "Play safe."

Uche refused to listen. Now as he watched the Liverpool game and saw the men in red stumbling their way about the pitch, he was horrified. What if these people actually lost? The game dragged on oppressively with the two teams throwing the ball about aimlessly. At half time Uche went to urinate nervously in his toilet. The second half began with more spirit. Ten minutes in and Liverpool scored a goal.

"Yes!" bellowed Uche, waking up his wife.

But the referee disallowed the goal and Uche cursed him heartily. The game continued and Uche was seating on the edge of his seat. Then Liverpool scored again and this time the goal was allowed. But just as Uche was counting his profits, the other team equalized much to his dismay. The game finally ran out and Uche stared hard at his slip, wishing he had listened to the advice of his friend and not played straight win.

Just then his wife came and gently reminded him of the children's school fees which was due on Monday. Uche nodded heavily and told his wife even though there was no money, he was sure God will provide. Then he went back to the toilet, tore up the slip, and bitterly flushed it down the drain. END

The Writer

124

Charles Kadib is a writer currently residing in the city of Port Harcourt. He has contributed pieces to the Metro review and the road to Dukana which was a tribute to Ken Saro Wiwa. He loves Artworks and movies and would release his first book next year.

Mobile: +2348038400767

Email: charleskadib@gmail.com

Facebook: Charles Kadib

The Funeral

by Obumneme Dominic Chukwu

Mme Jacques Cartier-Bertrand sat in a daze, her glassy eyes, red and swollen, staring at no one in particular. The salty stream of clear liquid pouring down her face was completely ignored, causing a wet patch on her black Yves Saint Laurent top that she wore. Her manicured fingers, splayed on her knees, tapped beats without rhythm as her thoughts tried to find some sense in all the chaos around her. She couldn't hear a word of what the good Père was saying, and she lacked the willpower to concentrate on the words coming from his lips. Those lips that had brought her uncountable delights and pleasure. Those lips that had worked wonders on her bare flesh as she tremulously attained peak after peak of pure erotic pleasure. Her drifting thoughts brought a cynic smile to her ashen face, which disappeared as quickly as it had come. Her gaze dropped back to the coffin.

***

M. François DE Chantal sat back among the congregation, observing the proceedings. He sat at the end of one pew, along the aisle, at the back. Due to the elevation at the back end of the church, he had a good view of the people gathered in the church. His interest was piqued by the number of people gathered to pay their last respects. But more importantly, the presence of the two men standing at the back unsettled him. They were dressed in black suits and black shoes. Their shades were even darker. Ordinarily, one would have thought they stood there because all the seats were filled up, but their unmoving stance filled him with trepidation. What would the French secret service be doing at the burial of a gambler? The dead guy owed his boss over ten million euros and he had been hired to retrieve the money. He was here to make sure the guy was not faking his death in order to abscond from his responsibility. Known locally as le grand meurtrier, the great killer, these guys won't hesitate to arrest him if his presence

126

was known. He made to stand up slowly to leave, but a hand came to rest on his shoulder, forcing him to sit back down.

***

She sang her heart away. It was the only cure she knew for her heartaches. Whatever emotional state she found herself in, she knew the songs to sing to make herself feel better. But even this time, her heart refused to budge. The choking sensation that had held her since she heard of his demise refused to let go. How would she, Sophie Angelique Vela live without him, she didn't know. He had been the center of her world. Twenty-four years of age and her heart refused to love any other. Thoughts of him brought smiles to her face often, and her diary had accumulated quite a number of poems and songs inspired by thoughts of him. Her world came to a crashing stop when she heard the news. She had taken off to his house to confirm the news, and seeing cars from sympathizers parked around the house confirmed the news to her. She couldn't bear to set foot into the abode, nor the courage to face his wife. She felt like she had been cheating on her with him, even though M. Cartier-Bertrand rarely looked at her twice. He always greeted her politely, but there's this twinkle in his eyes that always excited her. And that twinkle she thought of each time she touched herself in the bathroom as she showered. Fantasies painted in her mind and of which she wrote poems. Fantasies that would never be now that he's dead. She felt the choke hold her heart and plunged deeper into the solo she was singing.

***

The congregation stood, chanting hymns from the Hymnary distributed before the service commenced. A chorister will solo a verse and the church will respond with the chorus. Mlle. Marge Rapuntier, her name for today, stood scanning the crowd. Her job done when she walked by the corpse earlier, would have left the church, as was her MO. However, she was attracted by the young soloist currently singing, and her voice entrapped her with

127

its silky quality and at once she had envisioned an impassioned steamy session with the songstress. How good it would feel to have her sing afterwards, or in the shower, or whenever they cuddled. She preferred younger females and only had guys when she was working. Her most potent guile in her trade. Only that M. Cartier-Bertrand refused to fall for her antics. Refused to wind up in her bed. He really had her wondering if she was getting old, but yet each time he rebuffed her, albeit politely, she didn't find it difficult to pick up any man she wanted just to reassure herself. She had had him researched, to discover that the stinking rich guy had made his fortune dealing arms around the world. He sold to any party willing to buy. In fact, she had been hired to neutralise him by a party to a conflict that realized that, not only did he sell to the other side, he sold to them far cheaper than what they got the weapons for. Seventeen million dollars was the price, but her excitement wasn't from her impending account balance, she was far too preoccupied with the girl to think about the money. Maybe it's time for her to retire. No need to put the girl in harm's way. Retire and vanish with her. That she was the most lethal assassin and currently number one on Interpol's most wanted list would remain hidden from her. She bid her time as the priest got up to incense the casket.

***

The priest added incense to the censer and took it from the young altar boy. He approached the casket and made ready to pray over it. He prayed to God to grant the man a permanent, eternal rest, for he hated him. Père Simon hated the man in the casket for the distress he had caused his wife, Mme Jacques. He had known her over ten years now but about five years ago this man came and married her, interrupting their long-running affair. Père Simon had pleaded with her not to marry but she refused, because he himself had refused to leave the priesthood. And after the marriage, she refused to see the père for about a year, but when she came back, it was with a vengeance. The husband was always away, working as a pilot with the Doha headquartered Qatar airways. He spent months away at a time, but the few weeks he

128

was home were the longest and loneliest Père Simon would know. Most nights he would cry in his cold bed at the thought of his love in another's arms. But what pained him most was seeing her cry like this. He never believed she loved the pilot this much. And it was a relief to stand backing her now, so he wouldn't see her tear stained top. The tear drops had made the dress cling to her features, making the outline of her bra visible and giving him an erection on the altar. Holy fuck! God is so merciful the chasuble is free flowing, or his embarrassment would have been unbelievable! Men! He would need to see her soon to console her personally. And hopefully, this would be her last marital adventure.

***

The grey-haired man sat quietly in the pew. His face was showing the signs of wrinkling as he was getting on in years. He seemed to pay no attention to what was going on but actually missed nothing. He had seen the beautiful Argentine-born, Russian-trained, freelance assassin, for whom the burial had been set up. She was the most lethal Human alive and most evasive. But the dead man, a brilliant genius had come up with a plan to ensure she would be at his burial. It was a pity his best agent had insisted on resigning at such a very young age. He beat all other agents hands down in intelligence duties. All offers made to retain him had been declined and to stop him going, a bargain was made that should he be able to catch the female Carlos the Jackal, he would be allowed to retire. He had done that with flourish, and even threw in the local hitman for good measure. It seemed his greatest satisfaction in the whole scheme came from the natural end to the marriage with his cheating wife. Her affair with the priest had disgusted him a lot but gave him the impetus to stay longer on the job. He hated coming home. But still, he had found a small source of happiness in a beautiful young lady, the same one whom the feral jackal kept craning her head to look at from time to time. Normally she would have left, for the plan was to capture her outside the church as she left, but her lesbian side had kept her captive. Well, either way, she was never going to lay a hand on Sophie. She had been doomed from the time she showed up for the funeral.

***

Serenely he lay in the casket, unmoving. He would have loved to see how his funeral went, but some things were more important. Completely dead to the environment and people gathered, he found himself wandering in the dreamland, but the dreams weren't happy, because he could see his Sophie was very sad. And he couldn't console her. As for his wife, he couldn't care less if she committed suicide. He kept to her because he had a job to do. Other than that, he would have left ages ago. He had never talked to Sophie, other than to greet her, but he knew she loved him to bits. He saw it in her eyes. And he reciprocated by the twinkle each time he greeted her and hoped she noticed.

The risk involved in the job was such that they expected an attempt would be made to ensure he was dead. So, his suit, made by an agency tailor, had silk Kevlar between the suit material and the lining. Even his gloves were Kevlar. Which was well because hidden beneath the Jackal's manicured fingernail was a contraption loaded with a king cobra's venom. The Kevlar had prevented the delivery of this poison to his system, but he didn't know or feel anything.

***

Funeral service over, the hearse was carried out of the church. The mourners followed the pallbearers to the horse drawn carriage. Inside the casket, his finger moved. The tetrodotoxin from the puffer fish meal he had eaten earlier was beginning to wear off.

The Writer

A marine engineer by profession, became a writer as a hobby and now he is really enjoying telling stories.

Mobile: +2347031285521

Email: Chukwu.obumneme@gmail.com

Facebook: Chukwu Dominic

The Guest Who Did Not Know

by Oluwatosin Ebunoluwa Fatade

The famous chant that depicted an impending demonstration woke me from my nap one fateful afternoon. I had stayed over on campus with one of my friends so I could enjoy the uninterrupted power supply as exams were almost upon us. I read all night and up until a few hours into that morning. My eyes were red, partly from anger but more from having had my sleep cut short.

I stepped out of the room to listen to the address by the union representative; the Congress ground was directly opposite my friend's room, there was no way I could sleep through all that noise. Since I couldn't beat them, I did the needful.

I learnt that Saturday afternoon, that we students would refuse to participate in the exams starting the following week unless the results of the previous semester were first released. 'They can't be serious', I thought; the same exam I was slaving away for? A part of me knew I was the unserious party here, for two reasons: first, I wouldn't be slaving away now if I had been consistently reading and secondly, the union was not known to threaten or make vain protest declarations.

The union's "peaceful demonstration" was the most violent I had ever seen in all my 6 years at the university. The smell of burnt tires filled the air, my intestines growled in protest of the choking air and the yet again elongated years of study. It was my 6th year in the university studying a 5-year course - events happened in real time, I was preparing for the 2nd semester of 300 level and no I didn't fail at any point.

How the school Registrar was able to get a bulletin out amidst the chaos is commendable, they must have printed the notice of the umpteenth 'closure till further notice' from an outside location. The only lecturers I really sympathised with were the ones who needed to go for cleansing after being bathed with freshly-voided urine while discharging their duties dutifully.

I grabbed my bags and stuffed them with the few items that I had arrived with the previous day. I made for my rented apartment in town as quickly as possible to avoid the waterloo of soon to arrive red-beret officers. I met my roommate who didn't have an issue with candles still reading when I arrived my room. He was yet to get the memo. For a while, I wondered if I should let him continue reading or break the news to him. I chose the former as I couldn't recall any serious reading sessions he had that semester, it would do him some good. His phone was always switched off and dismembered at times like that when a crash-programme was underway. He was at my mercy, and I delivered him eventually the next morning. The punches I received that morning were not a few.

In the period of time our school last went on such an indefinite closure, my youngest uncle got married, put his wife in the family way and threw a big naming ceremony party before we were recalled. Neither myself nor my roommate was willing to return home, but we needed supplies - in lay terms, food! Going home was too unattractive as we would have to explain for the 7th time since admission, why we were home from school. I remember the look on my neighbour's face the last time, it was obvious she didn't believe my story. She must have told her son to start avoiding the dropout next-door. Their TV set must be broken or their family taboo was 'listening to news', I thought.

We still had food but it wouldn't have lasted a week especially as we had nowhere to go and nothing to do. A 2-minute call I received 3 days after the shutdown made the situation further depressing. A missionary who stayed with us every time he came to town for a crusade was at the other end of the line. The last time he came, I had assured him of our readiness to accommodate him at his next visit. "What would we do now?", Steven, my roommate asked. Couldn't God have informed him

133

that this is a bad time, that we are broke and hungry? Ignoring Steven's rhetoric, I considered cooking up an excuse for the man of God, and silently wished it would be one of those crusades where they had to fast all through!

In the weekend that followed, our guest arrived. Bro. Rejoice was unstoppable when it concerned sharing God's word and exploits and the different mighty works from his journeys. Steven and I independently wondered why God wouldn't do one of such exploits in our predicament. "The God I serve is able to and will do even so much more for you two who always accommodate me all the time", Bro. Rejoice prayed. I had never heard Steven say a louder 'Amen' in all my 6 years of knowing him. I countered with an even louder 'Amen' as if in a contest. Bro. Rejoice beamed at our response as Steven and I grinned knowingly to ourselves, if only he knew the hunger that was about to descend upon his soul!

That morning he arrived, we had just one large tuber of yam as the only food material in the room, along with some oil. I cooked it at noon, and shared it into 3 just as our guest was arriving from the morning session. Brunch is ready, I announced. Steven, who had been fake-sleeping jumped to life at the mention of food, while I also helped myself to what seemed to be our last meal. Bro. Rejoice was flipping pages of his Bible as we ate, he likes attending to his food only after the third invitation, I knew him for that. He'll reject your food or tell you not to worry the first 2 times and agree to eat as if not wanting to waste your efforts at the third. He never used more than 3 minutes to eat no matter the size and quantity of the food served, I remember timing him once or twice at his earlier visits. That day, I wasn't in the mood for repeated invitations, so I paused my hand mid-air on one of those hand to mouth trips and declared to him in the most assertive manner, "this yam is the only food available in this room this weekend and if you do not intend to fast through your forthcoming sessions, you had better start eating now!" I didn't realise what I had just mouthed as I left 3 adults shocked after my speech! He stopped flipping his Bible and started eating, 2

134

minutes and 40 seconds later, his plate was clean. It was Steven, not I who timed him.

We spent the succeeding 2 hours in the room in the most uncomfortable silence ever. I, on my part regretting my speech; my roommate disappointed and surprised I let the cat out of the bag and our guest sorry he bothered us. I was worried the man of God would return with food items after his next session, and I didn't want any of that. As Bro. Rejoice announced that he was leaving for the next session, my mouth got ahead again and I wished him a great time as I announced to him that I was joking the other time and it was only a prank to make him eat before the food got cold. I even bragged that a plate of beans and dodo would be waiting for him when he returned! Bro. Rejoice's wide smile bade farewell as Steven's inquisitive and unapproving stare welcomed me back to the room's reality. "It was bad enough that you spilled our predicament without tact, now you've totally created chaos with your promise", Steven said. Don't worry, the Lord will provide, I said. My intestines growled in mockery of my assertion, Steven laughed.

It was 6 pm and Bro. Rejoice was to arrive any moment from that time. In that moment, I regretted my lies. Had I not lied, Bro. Rejoice might show up with food and avert our imminent extinction. Approaching footsteps halted my thoughts, my heart accelerated as my brain surfed for recipes for another well-cooked lie. My heart skipped as the door knob turned but found its rhythm again when I saw Farouq make his way in. Farouq was Steven's course mate who was the only other student who stayed off campus in our street. He too had refused to return home but changed his mind after a week. Steven had no hesitations asking Farouq for help as they talked. That's one of the reasons I came, Farouq explained. I have foodstuffs that will be feasted on by rats and cockroaches before I return if I don't give them out. I came here to check if you guys were around so I could bring them, I really would hate to return to see them wasted.

It was that day I knew that God doesn't have to attend to a person's needs through someone of the same religion. Myself and

Steven dressed up and followed Farouq to the bounty, Mohammed did not have to come to the mountain, the mountains moved to the bounty!

That day, the Farouq I hardly exchanged more than greetings with became my friend too, not just Steven's. We returned with 2 paint buckets of rice, 1 of garri, 1 of beans, a sack of potatoes, 3 tubers of yam and one loaf of bread. And to my bewilderment, Farouq ran after us with a bowl in hand; a bowl he forgot to add to the bounty. It contained beans and dodo which his girlfriend had brought earlier but he decided not to eat as he was about to embark on a night journey home. I gave Steven a prophet's look; the Lord has provided I mouthed as Farouq ran off.

Later that night, Bro. Rejoice helped himself to a warmed plate of beans and dodo while we watched with empty plates of just devoured meals before us and filled hearts within us. And we ate happily ever after.

The end.

The Writer

I am a freelance writer and medical practitioner in Nigeria. An enthusiast for poems, short stories (fiction and nonfictional), public speeches and health related topics. I have poems and stories published on different blogs and own a blog at www.treasuredclaypot.com.ng

136

I believe Jesus Christ is saviour, I'm an optimist who sees the good in all and gives the benefit of doubt generously. My stories and work reflect my ideas and strong belief in love, goodness, hope, peace and justice.

Mobile: +2348059397898

Email: ebunfatade@gmail.com

Facebook: Tosin Fatade

LinkedIn: Tosin Fatade

Twitter: @TosinFatade

The Intersection

by Eunice Oladeji

These four whose destinies met at that one junction, at that one moment; none of them knew they were going to be at that spot at the same time with the other ones. It was a beautiful day, anybody would want to be outside but it ended in tragedy, leaving a frozen smile on the face of one of them who was left dead on the tarred road. This story shows the futility of life when considered from the perspective of more than one. One minute you think your life is perfect but you get to that point where it intersects with the supposedly perfect lives of others and you realise that life is just messed up. The girl, her boyfriend, the shop owner and the driver of the jeep make up a story that will never be forgotten.

***

I am the shop owner and I would be telling this story from my perspective. I always like sitting in my shop facing the window, looking at life through the plane window; people moving in different directions, some with smiles on their faces and others frowning as if the world had thrown bullets at them that they could not escape. It is always amazing to see that I could almost analyse the very lives of every person that walked across the window, many of them who took little or no notice of the man behind the window who could almost swear he could see through them. I was not so old but I had spent a lot of years in that town. So, I practically knew everybody.

I knew the woman who walked across the window at about 5 p.m. from her shop, going back to her children who would have been left in the house for hours on end without food. It wasn't like she did not care, she just was limited in how much she could offer for these little ones and I know about the man who was always in a black suit and a dark tie who always walked past my shop just 30 minutes after her. He was a single father. His wife had left him for someone richer. One would think that he was rich enough to have everything ever craved in the world but it was not so for him. His wife wanted more than he had so she left him and left the children. He would come home from office at about 5:30 p.m., stop by the restaurant near my shop, get plates of rice which he and the children would eat before they slept.

I also knew that beggar who sat in the market begging for alms, pouring prayers and blessings on everyone who passes by him in the hope of getting some money. I knew he was not lame for at the very end of the day, when everyone had retired to their homes, he would stand up, tall, proud and he would walk. Both legs functioning properly. It was his way of making life work for him and as long as his benefactors did not know he could walk, everything was fine.

I saw her walk by through the window of my shop again, the third time within the hour. She looked very nervous as she wrung the edge of her long scarf around her index finger. She would look across the road, try to stretch her neck over the bend and sigh, obviously not seeing who it was she was expecting. I was just the shop guy. It was not my business. She was not a regular customer of the shop. The few times she came, she was with her younger sister who always had to have a sweet before they left. Sweet little thing. I heard she died some months ago from what no one knew.

Her family had been the average family; average income, paying their bills and having enough money to eat and maybe put some clothes on their backs. They never had the luxuries of life but they were happy. Father, mother and the two daughters, looking at them from outside, one would wish to be a part of them. They had the loudest laughs and the widest and genuine smiles, always with a good word for anyone they met on the road. Theirs was the perfect family until things started going downhill for them.

First, the father lost his job. Any other person could have lost that job out of the hundred plus employees, why did it have to be their father? He was a good man, hardworking, diligent and very honest. Maybe the factory owner thought he was being funny when he decided to lay him man off. It struck a big blow

139

on the man and on the family's income. In the midst of his joy and carefree life, her father probably never thought about what would happen if he lost his job so they had no savings, nothing to fall back on considering that the wife was a full housewife. They could not pay their bills anymore and food became a luxury.

It did not take long before sickness came calling. It was first her mother who started coughing violently. This cough did not respond to the local herbs used in the town. She went to the local pharmacist who prescribed drugs for that temporarily relieved her of the cough. When the cough came back again, it came back like it was sent from the hell fire. Neighbours and relatives advised that she be sent to the local hospital where she could be taken care of properly but there was no money to do so. She kept coughing till blood poured from her mouth like a tap. This was when the family realized this cough was very serious but it was too late. She died and left the disease with her husband. He did not even last as long as she did. His body had already been battered by the bottles of beer he got across the street after he lost his job. The blood from his mouth came barely a week after he started coughing. He was too frail, too fragile, too weak to even fight the way his wife had fought. Concerned neighbours had taken the sisters out of the house to protect them from the disease.

A year had passed since their parents died when one morning, she woke up and found her sister dead on the bed, just beside her. The cold feel of her sister's dead body on her skin probably triggered her psychiatric break down. She screamed and kept screaming for hours on end. The kind neighbours who had taken them in took her to the psychiatric doctor at the local hospital. They gave her drugs and injections, they even put wires on her head to shock the psychiatric disease out of her body. None of those things worked. She said she could see her parents and her little sister talking with her, beckoning for her to join them in the life after. Everyone at the hospital had given up on any recovery for her. Till he came around.

140

He was the son of one of the nurses in the hospital. He had walked by her room when he came to see his mother on his way back to school. She did not know him from anywhere but when he walked past her door, she called his name and unlike every other person, he did not cringe or seem afraid. He walked into her room and started talking with her. After he came back from school about a month later, he started visiting her regularly, singing for her, playing his guitar and making her laugh. The improvement was amazing. Soon enough, the doctor decided she was well and fit to be discharged from the hospital. The young man had spoken with his mother and he was convinced that he wanted to live with this beautiful angel who life had been unfair to. His mother agreed as she knew the lady was a very good girl who would make her son even happier than he was already. He had gone back to school for a few more months and was coming back to take her along with him to become man and wife.

She had stopped pacing. She was looking at him, a young man with a guitar slung across his left shoulder, waving at her with his right hand. Smiling. I could imagine she was smiling too as she crossed the road to meet him.

Did the smile remain on her face after her head hit the tarred road? Did the drunk driver of the black jeep see that smile before he hit her? What of the young man across the road? Did he cherish that last smile?

This time last year, I saw futility. She was the only one left. Her parents died from an unmentionable disease. Her sister, cause of death unknown. And she?

A smile splattered on the tarred road.

The Writer

Eunice Oladeji is the third of four children born to a Christian family from Osun state, Nigeria. She is currently a final year medical student in the University of Ibadan. She enjoys reading, writing, speaking, singing and making people laugh. Her love for writing has brought out many stories, articles and poems. She has a personal blog (princess139@wordpress.com) and also works for The DesignedLife blog and The SpotLight blog.

Mobile: +2347064900756

Email: theozinyjoel@yahoo.com

Facebook: Eunice Oladeji

Instagram: Eunice Oladeji

Twitter: @euniceoladeji

THE MOMENT

by Edikan Kinza

11:01 AM

The sun was up ahead yet the ground was cold. Birds circled in the sky above. Dancing, diving and getting lost in the veil of cloud then reappearing in another while I watched, my body too heavy to move. Dizzy and weak, eyelids fluttering every minute, their song sent me to sleep- a long spiral sleep.

11:15 AM

A loud cry awoken my senses. My heart beat raced and my head ached like I had been run over by a hundred horses. I tried to get up but the pain in my legs got worse. Alone in my misery but for a sparrow perched on the tree keenly watching my every move. I shifted to the side and gathered what was left of my strength then I sat up. A few minutes later, my little companion flew away to join the others. So much for loyalty.

11:30 AM

My legs had been badly hurt, still determined, I limped towards the village seduced by the sound of drums. Celebration or commotion? It was hard to tell. I hid in the bush, quietly parting the leaves. The air felt thick and suddenly Eno was behind me. "It's too late", he said, before briskly walking away. Alone again, I peeked from my cover. The village was spread out before me yet the silence was deafening.

11:35 AM

Vultures were circling around a woman. Some had gathered on the ground to gnaw at what she held in her hands- what seemed to be flesh. I couldn't tell. The woman shooed the animals away and they moved a few paces back.

I squinted and covered my nose as smoke made its way towards me. Laughter emanated from the hut and I cowered but couldn't stop myself from sneezing.

"Who's there?" was all I heard as I scampered away from the scene and back the way I came. My heart fluttered and I looked back from a safe distance, confused and out of shape. I felt the ground shake beneath me. It all happened in a minute. I tumbled and landed near the rock. That was when I woke up.

11:02 AM

The sun was still up ahead. Birds circled in the sky above me. My head ached like I had been run over by a hundred horses. I couldn't move my legs. They were badly hurt but I managed to shift a little. Indeed, the ground was cold and when I turned sideways to see Eno lying beside and coldly staring at me, I understood why.

The Writer

Edikan is a Writer and a Lover of the Arts. She believes that there is no limitation to that which can be achieved through oral and written expression of thoughts. She hold a Bachelor of Agriculture-Animal Science degree (University of Uyo) and Master of Science degree in Environmental Toxicology and Pollution Management (University of Lagos). She loves music and enjoy watching football. It is her desire to be a renowned source of inspiration with a voice and a force to be reckoned with on the global stage. She is currently the creative consultant on treasureinhearts.com which is an inspirational blog aimed at satisfying every inspirational need.

Email: ekongedikan@gmail.com
Facebook: Edikan.Kinza
Instagram: @edikan_kinza
Twitter: @edykinza

The Other Tent

by Nifemi SOLA-OJO

I

The morale in the Lafia Dole army command centre was as high as the temperature inflicted by the Northern Nigeria scorching sun. The previous day had been a tremendous victory for the men and women, stationed at the fronts to fight the insurgents troubling the peace of the nation. Two Infantry Units went out in place of men of the Artillery to act on intelligence received almost a week ago. The well-known terrorist sect was using a village southeast of the base as a cover, knowing fully-well we would never be able to attack because of the possible casualties a siege could cause. This fact troubled members of my unit. Sending terrorists to their early graves was our job and at that time we couldn't do our jobs. This made us sad.

People like to call me "Cap", short form for Captain. My men often assembled in small groups to have small talks and occasionally, they'd look at me with some expression I can't really describe.

The Platoon Sergeant finally came to me and spoke with his gaze on my feet

"Cap, what we are going to do about these cowards using women and children as shield?" paused for a few seconds and added "Sir!"

I couldn't give any response. I felt inadequate as a leader.

I realized it wasn't going to hurt to try to talk to the base commander about the situation again. Getting to his tent, he was calmly smoking his cigar and gently having his scotch like always. I wondered how someone could find so much pleasure in smoking in the weather condition, but wondering wasn't what I was there do, I was there to tell sweet Colonel my plan.

At the beginning of my explanation, he already knew where I was taking my speech and he interrupted me promptly

"Hey, Mister Man", you are not the only one concerned about these girls, we all are. I have direct orders from my superiors to stand down for as long as it takes and as long as there are women and children used as cover in that village. Just like I am religiously following the instruction of my commanding officer you will obey mine too. Is that clear?"

"Yes sir!" I replied putting up an act of a disciplined officer.

I had no intention of standing down. On my way back to my tent I continued talking to myself, mocking and mimicking the Colonel

"Hey Mister Man, weh yeh weh yeh..."

Speaking like some toddler just learning to speak properly. Then I replied in my actual voice in response to Colonel calling me Mister Man.

"It is not Mister, Colonel. It is Captain" I heard some footsteps, someone was approaching and I was silent, looked around, it wasn't the colonel and I completed my discussion with myself.

My men were waiting and hoping for some good news. I signaled at the two Sergeants. They gathered their men and we met far away from the Colonel's tent.

They assembled at once, fixing all their gazes on me. It was time to give one of those speeches I have rehearsed alone in my tent.

I began what was going to be the best speech of my life

"I know what they taught you at Depot and I remember what I learned in NDA too, but today is not about our training, it is about our conscience.

Can we really sit on our hands and wait while some people keep daughters and sisters away from their homes just because we were told to stay put?

147

I imagine having a daughter of mine someday and someone grabs her from her school, and then keeps her in some known remote village while I lay awake every night uncertain about the welfare of my girl. There are a lot of parents, relatives and friends of these girls out there lying awake right now, unsure of the fate of their loved ones and here we are, staying put and standing down because we were told to do so.

I will never ask you to do anything that will bring you dishonour. On a day like this, it will be impossible for me to be a good soldier and also a good man at the same time. A good soldier will follow the instructions of his superior. I am not asking you to be a soldier today; I am begging you to be a father, to be a brother, I am begging to be a man. Join me; let us get these girls back to their homes.

I will not judge you if you step aside because this is what a good soldier would do and believe me this country need a lot of good soldiers.

Today, you get to be just one, either a good man or a good soldier."

There was no need to ask any questions, seeing their faces I knew these men were ready to send some terrorists back to their makers that night.

I gave the final instruction

"We assemble at 03:45hrs gear up and be ready for combat. If anyone asks you any questions, tell them it is just a drill. Is that clear?"

"Yes sir!" The two platoon sergeant with a solid nod.

A good speech won't bring the girls back home. I needed a plan, not just a plan but a very good plan. A plan that will get my men back at the base in one piece and the girls safely to their homes.

Less than a kilometre away from us, an Air Force Intelligence Unit was stationed to support the army troops with communications and surveillance. I had previously volunteered to fill in for a sick system analyst in the system communications and security unit at the Air force command centre, when a young officer had to be sent home after being suspected to have a very contagious flu.

I made a lot of friends in the Air Force Comm. Unit. While I was filling in for the Systems Analyst, I also doubled as a programmer.

For a few weeks until the replacement came, I worked day and night with Air force officers gathering intelligence both for the country and covertly for my team.

I had saved a few pictures from the surveillance feeds just to study the villages nearby. I pulled up these pictures. The abductors were often routinely not prepared for combat between 5:00hrs and 6:00hrs. They were always gathered at some sort of entrance to the village. We will have to divide the men into two units. Alpha unit will go and find the girls and Bravo unit will engage the insurgents and prevent them from interfering with the rescue.

It was a simple and clean plan. In my experience, no mission ever goes as planned.

At the Airforce command centre, someone was my breath of fresh air in the midst of all the craziness. Flight Lieutenant Mary Omali, Drone Pilot. I called her to ask for her assistance by running ops for us from their base. She could do that in her tent alone, all she would need is a drone controller and a terminal to see the feeds captured by the drones.

I asked her how long that would take, she said she already did.

I was a bit puzzled "So, you have a mini Operational Command Centre in your room, Lieutenant?"

She replied

"We are the eyes in the sky baby and I always watch you. I saw you gather your men a few hours ago after speaking with the Colonel; I figured you just grew some balls and you were going to need my help"

I was speechless and when I finally found my voice I said

149

"You are going to be my ears and eyes tonight then?"

She replied and I could tell she was smiling when she said

"No, Captain. I am going to be your guiding angel!"

Flight Lieutenant Mary Omali is one of the most brilliant ladies I have meant in my entire life, military or civilian. Believe me; I have met a lot of ladies. She wasn't shallow, she was smart and beautiful. If I was normal, I would say I was in love.

II

04:00hrs Rendezvous location

If bravery had a smell, it smelled just like us. I relayed my plan to my team; everyone knew where to be and what to do. Going over the plans again because some of my men can be a little slow at times, we were distracted by the sound of a truck coming from our rear. I signaled for everyone to split into their units and take cover.

Emerging from the dust raised by the vehicle was Lieutenant Omali.

My men recognized her because she had been on our base more than a few times to see me. We would write some C codes in my tents for the drones and discuss a lot about trends in Computer Science and Programming. She often teased me about how often I couldn't read most of her Assembly Language codes. That was all we did, talk about computer science and coding. My men refused to believe that all I did was write computer codes for long hours alone with a pretty lady in my tent. I am not obliged to convince anyone what I do in the other tent.

My men stood up in one accord and saluted her as she approached; she saluted back told them to be at ease. The men continued giggling, I gave a scolding stare and they stopped at once.

I dragged her aside

150

"Jesus good Christ, what on God's green earth are you doing here Lieutenant, you are supposed to provide support from your base. You shouldn't be here"

She seemed to have a good response for me.

"And why shouldn't I be here oh, Mister...?"

I knew this was going with all the sarcasm. So, I told her like I have a thousand times

"First, it is not Mister..."

She interrupted and continued my sentence in an attempt to sound like me

"...it is Captain and if that is too long you can call me Cap."

We couldn't repress the laughter.

She had a rifle with her. I knew if I told her she was to support the men from the safety of her base because she is a lady, I'd probably get shot, so I kept my opinion to myself.

She is a very fast speaker. She started with a detailed explanation on why she could be with us dressed for combat too, and not staying in front of a computer to monitor movement in the villages and give us updates in real time.

"Remember that day I came with my laptop to your tent?"

I nodded to confirm.

She continued

"And we wrote a script to automate the processes and tasks a drone pilot will have to do to keep drones in flight and at the same time maintain focus on subjects under surveillance?"

She paused, waiting for me to confirm that I in fact remember. With some sort of grin on my face, I replied

"Oh, I remember that"

She hit me to whisk me out of my thoughts.

All we did that day wasn't just code by the way.

She handed everyone a communication device and said

"With these little babies, we will all be able to hear ourselves. Try not to talk all at once so we can hear ourselves properly"

Everyone was in position before we could advance, Lieutenant Omali was alerted by a beep on her PDA and she saw a footage showing the insurgents splitting into two groups for no reason at all. The other group decided to have their prayers at the far end of the village.

Mary suggested another plan.

Alpha Team (Lead by Flight Lieutenant Omali)

They went in to get the girls. Bravo and Delta Teams covered from two opposite ends.

Bravo Team (Lead by Capt. Musa Adamu aka Cap)

They engaged the terrorists close to the front entrance of the village, cutting them off and allowing the Alpha team to safely evacuate the girls.

Delta Team (Lead by Staff Sergeant Olusola)

They attacked the terrorists at the back entrance, preventing them from interfering with the rescue.

At the end of the mission, most of the terrorists were shot and killed, while others fled the village.

Everyone got out in one piece except for Lieutenant Omali, she had used her body as a shield, to prevent one of the girls from getting shot. She got shot twice.

The high morale and celebration at the base didn't get to me, I was lost in my thoughts and I couldn't clear the picture of Mary covered in blood in my head. It was as if the whole world was still.

She is in surgery; the medical staffs at the base have been trying to revive her. She lost a lot of blood. I lay awake wondering what is going to happen to my girl.

The room is becoming blurry because of the tears in my eyes. It's been days.

Finally, the doctor came to my tent and said she was going to be fine, that I could go see her in the morning when she wakes. I went to stay at her bedside immediately. I waited for her to open her eyes like a watchman waited for dawn.

When she did open her eyes, I felt like I was walking on water. I couldn't hold back my ear-to-ear smiles and neither could I do anything about my tears.

After being unconscious for days, I'd assumed she won't have the time to still pick on me and all she did was to say

"Don't cry, Mister"

Then and there I knew I was going to do anything humanly possible to spend the rest of my life with her.

III

I was scheduled for trial on the counts of disobeying my superior's orders and also falsifying the order of a superior officer. I told the jury I had lied to my men and Lieutenant Omali, telling them that I was acting on the instructions of the Colonel and the will of the president.

I emphasized that my men as far as they were concerned, thought they were carrying out the instructions of the Base commander.

I was discharged from the army and stripped of my ranks.

My men and Lieutenant Omali were awarded medals of honour for gallant acts in combat.

She never called me Mister again; instead, she calls me husband.

The Writer

Nifemi SOLA-OJO works mostly with tech startups as a Software Engineer but he comes to life when he writes fiction. He graduated from Federal University of Technology Minna, with a Bachelor of Technology in Library & Information Technology in 2014 and he is currently pursuing a post-graduate degree in Computer Science at University of Lagos. Follow him on twitter at @Capt_Nigeria

Mobile: +2347033278594

Email: nifemisolaojo@ymail.com

Facebook: nsolaojo

Twitter: @Capt_Nigeria

154

The Reason

by Maggie Smart

ONE

Mary

Mary stomps out of her house angrily and sits on the little stone just by the door. She calls it her 'thinking stone' but there is no thinking being done at that moment. She is so angry, she can't think straight and she has nowhere else to go. Joseph is out of town for a job and she doesn't feel like seeing Rebecca, her best friend, just now.

How can her mum insist she is pregnant? She cannot be pregnant as no man has ever touched her including Joseph, her fiancé. She has not as much as kissed him not to mention doing any other thing. She can't even think about it.

She who has insisted to Joseph she would like to keep her virginity till marriage. Although they are technically married, bless his soul, he has agreed and has told her he had never intended to touch her before the final marriage rites anyway, and that her decision is fine with him. She still thanks God for blessing her with a man such as Joseph.

Although many of their friends are having sex, and the ladies certainly know of a way to avoid pregnancy or unplanned children would be the norm, she has decided right from when she was twelve that she would never indulge in such acts, she has resolved to keep her body for the man she is going to marry. Thankfully, that man is Joseph, who never pressures her for sex.

She makes short order of the walk to Rebecca's house, her long robe sweeping the floor as she goes along. "I don't know why we have to wear such long gowns, can't we just make do with ankle length and be done with it? Then, we wouldn't have to worry about washing clothes with filthy ends every other day. Oh well, nothing can be done about fashion." She thinks to herself.

She looks up just then and sees Rebecca waving to her from the fields to the right of their property. Mary skips to meet her.

"What are you doing here? I thought we weren't meeting today?" Rebecca asks.

"Plans changed. I had to see you."

Rebecca looks closely at Mary and sees she looks a bit peeved. "What's wrong?" she asks, and moves closer.

"You wouldn't believe what my mother did this afternoon." Mary begins.

Rebecca rolls her eyes. "What did she do again? You are always getting into little arguments with your mother. You have to remember the law of Moses that says we should honor our parents, Mary."

"Oh well, that's neither here nor there." Mary says with a dismissive wave. "When I tell you what she did, you'll definitely take sides with me."

"Okay, let's hear it then."

Mary puts on a dramatic look and moves nearer to Rebecca as if to whisper a secret. "She said I am pregnant."

Rebecca's hand flies to her mouth. "Noooooooo" she says, her eyes wide with disbelief.

"Yes." Mary affirms, nodding her head enthusiastically.

"Why did she say that?"

Mary shrugs. "I don't know."

"Do you feel pregnant?" Rebecca asks peering at her.

"What sort of question is that? Of course, I don't feel pregnant. You have to have sex to get pregnant,

and I didn't, so, end of discussion."

156

"Okay, okay. I just had to ask."

Mary suddenly remembers a certain dream/vision she has had just a little while ago where an angel appears to her and tells her she will be made pregnant by the Holy Spirit. She has dozed off one afternoon while helping her mother sort some barley and she has had a dream where an angel appears to her and tells her these things.

She can't really classify it as a dream because she is semi-aware of her surroundings when it happens but she wakes up as if she has been dreaming. In the dream, the angel also tells her that Elisabeth, her cousin is expecting a baby. This is astonishing because Elisabeth is an old woman and they have lost all hope that she would ever have any child with Zachariah. Maybe I'll pay them a visit just to be absolutely sure. Mary decides.

Can it be that this is how it would happen? She has assumed God would at least wait until she is properly married before carrying out his plan. Has it happened already? Mary pushes these thoughts to the back burner of her mind. She'd rather not think about the implications of getting pregnant out of wedlock.

"Please, let's talk about something else. I have heard enough of pregnancies for one day."

They stroll arm in arm through the field and talk all the way; about parents, boys and their friends who are being naughty.

***

So, it has finally happened. How can God do this to her when he knows what happens to women presumed to have committed adultery? Here she is, pregnant, without a husband, still living with her parents and all because of a dream she is not sure is not a figment of her imagination.

All these thoughts war in Mary's mind as she lays on the palette staring at the ceiling. Her eyes are shut tightly. She does not dare look at her mother, she doesn't want to see the knowing look on her face. She has finally succumbed to her mother and allows her do the test just to shut her up. She had thought she has nothing to hide, apparently, she was wrong.

Suddenly, she jumps up from where she lays and bounds to the door. Her mother grabs her arm before she can move further.

"And where do you think you are going, wayward child?" Anne asks.

Mary winces. She feels she deserves that. After all, here she is with a pregnancy that is difficult to explain and about to bring shame on her family. Who would believe her when she says an angel appeared to her and told her she would get pregnant by the Holy Spirit? Everyone will just assume she is promiscuous and she will be stoned to death for adultery. Even Joseph would not believe her. How do you explain the impossible?

"I just want some air, mother."

"No, no, no. You are going nowhere until your father gets back."

"Okay mother." Mary agrees and goes to sit dejectedly at the corner. She supposes it's bye-bye to freedom of movement from that point on. Now, she has to account for every moment of her day.

"Jehovah, you have to take control. Save me from this, teach me, and above all, let your will be done." she prays.

TWO

Joseph

Joseph is confused. He has just come from Mary's house and he has heard the most baffling news. Mary is pregnant and naturally, the blame falls on him. After all, he is her betrothed. Definitely, they think he's responsible hence, the summons. A messenger has come to him just this evening asking him to come down to Mary's house. He has rushed along, hoping nothing has happened to Mary, only to be told this.

It is clear to both Mary and Joseph that nothing untoward happened between them. Then, how do they explain the pregnancy? Can it be that Mary has been unfaithful? Joseph doesn't want to think that. Mary is a good woman with the fear of God. It is hard to imagine her being cunning enough to string along two different men.

There must be a logical explanation to this and not the laughable one Mary tells them this evening. A pregnancy by the Holy Spirit? It is quite obvious she is just looking for an explanation to the mess she finds herself in. The thought is as far-fetched as it is impossible.

Nothing can be done about it though. They'd have to break their engagement but it will be done quietly so as not to bring ridicule on her. He knows what happens to women caught in this situation and he loves Mary too much to allow such happen to her. According to the law, women caught in adultery are stoned to death and this situation is dead on. An unexplainable pregnancy and a betrothed who knows he is not responsible. Maybe they can pull it off, maybe it can be done without dire consequences. Maybe, just maybe.

That night, Joseph has a dream that totally changes the tide of things. In the dream, an angel appears to him and confirms everything Mary says. According to the angel, she is indeed

159

pregnant by the Holy Spirit and it is for the fulfillment of God's words.

Somehow, he has been chosen to be the father to the son of the Highest God. He, a sinner, who tries to love God and walk according to his precepts but falls short often, has been chosen to do this all-important task. Joseph is filled with awe at the power of God. Nothing is impossible for God, even getting a virgin pregnant without intercourse.

He is glad he doesn't have to break his engagement with Mary because a good woman like that, who loves God and is ready to obey him, is hard to find.

What remains to be done now is to make arrangements to have the marriage rites completed so Mary can come to his home as his wife.

THREE

Mary

Few months later

Mary can't believe she is married. The latest events in her life have been very trying and she has all but ruled out thoughts of marriage. What man wants to marry a woman who is pregnant with a baby that's not his? It just shows how good a man she has in Joseph; God-fearing and just in his dealings with everyone. Mary is ecstatic.

They are in Bethlehem for the census and Mary is excited to see Joseph's home town. Although she is heavy and will soon put to bed, she knows they can still make it back in time before the baby comes. Little does she know that she is in for a big surprise.

By the time they come into Bethlehem, everywhere is packed full with people. They can't get a room in any inn as they were all full. After searching and searching with no result, they see a manger by the road and decide to manage it, just for the night.

Joseph gathers some straw and makes it into a bed for Mary to lie on. The straw is not enough for two beds so he lies on the floor beside her and they go to sleep.

A few hours later, Mary goes into labor and Joseph is terrified, he has no idea what to do. He has always assumed that when the time comes, there will be women around to help his wife through the labor, but alas, the task falls to him and he doesn't know the first thing about childbirth.

"Mary, can you hold on till morning? So, I can get help?" he asks while pacing around watching her pant.

"I don't think this baby will wait till morning Joseph. The pain is too much."

"Oh. So sorry." He keeps pacing, frantically wishing for daybreak.

He rushes to her side as her screams rent the air. He is watching her face intently when he hears a faint cry underneath her whimpers. He searches for the source of the sound and sees the tiny human just between her legs.

"He's here. He's here. Mary, Jesus is here." He shouts, jumping up for joy and laughing joyously.

He carries the child, cleans him up and wraps him in some clothes to keep him warm before attending to his wife.

After Mary is cleaned up, she cradles her son in her arms and looks into his eyes. "The son of God is here to bring salvation to the world." She declares

And thus, it begins.

The Writer

My name is Bolu-Adebayo Margaret and I write under the pseudonym Maggie Smart. I'm the second of three children in a family of five. I attended University of Ilorin and bagged a bachelor's degree in Chemistry in 2011, then I proceeded to earn a post-graduate diploma in Journalism in 2013.

I have been writing for five years now. I published my first novel in 2012, and since then, I have published another novel and three novellas. I love writing and I am working at sharing my gifting with the world.

Mobile: +2348066850649

Email: maggiesmartscribes@gmail.com

Facebook: Maggie Smart

Instagram: @maggiesmartauthor

Twitter: @wummyy

Uloma's mushrooms

by Ugochukwu, Evans, Nwankwo

(1a)

Mama spread the mat gently on the ground. Her calloused hands draped the surface with expertise — not a crease, not a fold. She sat on the 'story stool' — a beige wooden stool in its centenary. Mama had told me, my great grandfather — her father, made it the day she was born. He was a master craftsman like my father. Mama was very fond of him "his hands were as hard as wood, when he would lift me, and place me on his lap, it was like sitting on an Iroko tree. But when he spoke, his voice — it was soft and mellifluous like a wood warbler poised on Ugwele mountains. It took me through forests and anthills, guided me through realms and kingdoms, love and battles, of beings, of nature, and elements," Mama would go on and on. I'd never met him, but his surreal existence under a cashew tree beside our old house, seemed to captivate me often, until the mud cracked, and our old house had toppled over. Father had ended my intermittent sojourns with a barricade of palm fronds. The civil war was one of her favorite stories as well. "It was a very dark time," she had said, I could only imagine — a time when meat was so rare, that lizards had been a most comforting delicacy for Father, and there was rustling everywhere. The civil war had stolen their home, and our great grandfather had come to Elele, to stay with Mama. He'd never left since then.

The wooden door behind us flew open, as other children skipped lightly towards us, in a frenzy of excitement. Chidi and Chisom — my uncle's daughters, with their hands joined, and their ponytails bobbed up and down, like a seesaw. Then came running Kosara, bearing remnants of his dinner — roasted yam, and palm oil. Ignoring his sisters, he scrambled beside me on the mat, his legs snaked like a Buddhist. Tone, Cheta and Ikenna appeared next, giggling mischievously, their moist skin glittering in the moonlight, redolent with mosquito repellant. My two elder sisters entered, chewing gum, and making it pop. I wondered what they were doing here — if they were too old to play with Soma and me, then they shouldn't be here either. A cursory glance from Mama made them spit the gums on the ground, as they slightly cowered on the mat. Soma was the last to appear, his white pajamas greatly emphasized his ebony skin. If he stripped right there, he would blend nicely in the dark. Had we not shared Fathers round face, and fragile frame, nobody could guess we were born on the same day.

When all ten of her grandchildren were ensconced on the mat, Mama smiled broadly, a twinkle appeared in her eyes, and a dimple on her sagging cheeks — how I loved to pull her cheeks, sometimes a little too hard to make them wobble, although she always pretended not to like it. Magnificent stars dazzled above, adding to the luminous intensity of the moon. The air was dry and chilly, gnawing through our bones like gliding knaves.

A great hush descended. Ears twitched, and waved in anticipation. Mama began.

"Story story."

"Story," we responded.

"Once upon a time."

"Time, time," we echoed in timely fashion.

Soon, her voice took on the brilliant cadence of a refined raconteur.

"Far away, a long time ago, in the land of Abor, a very beautiful damsel called Uloma was caught between two men, between love and sacrifice. One, her heartthrob, the other chosen by her family, her king, and her people. They left her with no choice. There remained only one thing to do, to free herself, and the one she loved. Now listen to how it went down."

(2a)

165

Uloma bent to pick up the bruised cherry she had just plucked. The strung beads around her shapely waist clapped harmoniously like a sonorous harp. She cut a twig, using the leaves to wipe the white smear off her straight legs. She paused suddenly, her full lips drawn in a look of alarm. Was someone watching her? She had heard something in the bush a distance away. She recalled she had felt the same way earlier in the morning, when she went to the river to bath. She had just removed her bodice, and her creamy breasts had stood like calabashes, pointing to the pear tree which provided her shade. Splash! A stone had fallen into the river, but who had thrown it? She had quickly jumped into her clothing, and as she glanced around furtively on her way home, she knew she was not alone. Now, ever so familiar, creeping doubts assaulted her. Was she paranoid? Emeka was running late, she thought he would be there as always to welcome her when she arrived. Then she would lie with her head on his lap, and he would stroke her hair, her face — his hands were so gentle, then he would sing to her.

"Emeka! Emeka." She shouted, but nobody responded. It wasn't him hiding in the bushes, ready to chase her around the cherry tree, and peel the bark of the tree where he carved his heart — his love. It wasn't him. Uloma gathered her strength, and ran. She did not look back this time.

(2b)

All the maidens had gathered at the palace courtyard. It was the great dance festival. Prince Opi would finally chose his bride, before succeeding his father. The entire palace was swarming with feminine activities. The Sleek, frail, corpulent; women with broad chest like watermelons, and tall like palm trees, all vying for his attention. He was disappointed. She wasn't there. He had scanned through the maidens, one after other, she wasn't there. He had removed the polished bronze from his head, his eyes hurt, his head too.

Why wasn't she here?

166

Ekwe — the town crier surely did not make mistakes.

Who was she to defy him?

Did she think she was better than him?

It had taken all his strength not to approach her at the river, and when his guards had returned, he had dismissed them again, while he sat beside the cherry tree. He already knew her house. He signaled a palace guard, whispered into his ear, and sent him away.

(2c)

Uloma was behind the hut. Her slender hands flashed elegantly around the raffia. Beside her lay two brown mats, beautifully made. She didn't hear her enter.

"Uloma, what are you doing while everyone is at the palace?" Caught unawares, she turned, "Mama Chinwe, I hope all is well."

"The maidens are about to begin their dance, and you're asking if all is well?" She shook her head. "I only came here because your mother has requested your presence."

"Tell her I'm not coming."

"Tell her yourself," she pulled her up to her feet. "Your mother was taken to Ejiji." Uloma's anger soon turned into agitation, "what! When?" She flustered around. Uloma wiped her hands, and quickly ran out of the compound. "Mama please don't leave me, you're all I've got."

(1b)

"It was a trick, a malicious ploy to get her to the palace." Mama looked down at us, one at a time, as if to let the words sink. Then she continued.

(2d)

No sooner had she arrived, when a palace guard forced her into the dance. Uloma stood, not moving a muscle. The maidens flowed, and gyrated around her, like spirit dancers of the high priestess, until the music stopped. It was most surprising then, when she was chosen. Her perplexity grew even more, as she sat beside the Prince two days later for the marriage ceremony, and coronation. Her tears ignored, her rebuffs waved aside. He always stared at her with lust. Her mother, she was not hurt after all, but she had joined the people to celebrate her. They wouldn't let her leave.

Why wouldn't they stop?

Emeka, where was her hero — the great hunter?

Why wouldn't he rescue her?

The crowd cheered. It was over. She was his.

(2e)

Uloma's teeth rattled in the dark as she waited for him under the tree. She drew comfort from familiar settings. She had slipped out at night during the royal gathering. She had complained of a headache, and the Prince who had been flaunting his prize all day long had excused her. She needed rest after all, for what was to come that night. Then she heard his voice, strident like an eagle, he enveloped her in his arms. She rested her head on his chest, and sighed. His knees buckled as they both fell. His face was drawn and sallow. His voice was almost a whisper, then she saw his abdomen — the angry slash of flesh, the tilting flow of blood — like old vine. She recognized that wound, it was an angry slash from the claws of a carnivore. His last words "Uloma," he whispered, "I..."

She screamed, it erupted like a volcano, a furnace of anger blazing through the forest. Then it was over. Still. They seemed to beckon on her, she knew what they meant; she understood. The elements, nature, they spoke to her. Such grief they felt. She heeded their call with great difficulty, she plucked two mushrooms, discerning their efficacy — prolonged maybe, but they would do. She squeezed, then ate them raw. Soon, the pain

168

increased, searing through her stomach like fire. They were called 'bitter mushrooms' for a reason. She embraced the pain, as she gathered him in her arms, then she stared up, above the cherry tree, far above the receding moonlight and the sky, into the undulating clouds of daylight.

(1c)

Soma snored lightly, his head was crooked at one angle. They were all asleep. I tugged at my shorts as I looked up at Mama, then I hugged her. With a note of melancholy, I spoke, "Mama, would you make me some mushroom soup tomorrow?"

She nodded. "Anything for you my dear child."

The Writer

Nwankwo Ugochukwu Evans is a seasoned writer, instructor, and motivational speaker. His works have been shortlisted for the Rusty Scythe awards, and long listed for the Writivism Koffi Addo prize. He has appeared on literary shows like 'children readers club.' When he is not touring Nigeria for literary workshops, or jotting down words at a corner, he can be found in the lab, testing his knowledge as a Biochemist."

Mobile: +2348061173651

Email: evansmenu@gmail.com

Facebook: Ugochukwu Markevans

We Are God's Little Mistakes

by Victor Daniel

If you ask Jane about me, she would heave a huge sigh that has regrets, emptiness and raw anger dripping from the exhale. She would look at you with her face contorted into a frown. The perpetual glint that always shone in her eyes would vanish, and her eyes would slowly transform into a fog. She would shake her head slowly, and chuckle, and tell you about the boy who could not be loved. 'That boy', she would say, poking your chest with her forefingers, 'is the Devil'. She would make a great show of it, her hysteria fueled by the reminiscence of the nightmare that I was to her, and she would grit her teeth in a renewed show of regret while she tries to make you understand why I am more dangerous than I appear. She would stagger backwards and flop on the seat behind her, using both hands to draw gestures in the air as she explains to you how the butterflies inside of me were dead and were replaced with poisonous moths with cold feet. She would tell you about the boy who swayed to her house like an empty paper-box dancing in the wind every evening to eat noodles and make love to her and sneak out in the morning before anyone else woke up like though he was leaving a place he was not supposed to be.

She would bite her lips in regrets, and tell you about the distance in my eyes when she stared into them, and the internal constriction she felt was going on inside of me every time she hugged me tight. 'I didn't know what it was', She would say, glass-eyed, 'but it was like he was ashamed of something. Of me or of himself'. Then she would pause, and swallow, and continue—'but I hate that he did not leave when he should have. I hate that he stayed and tried to comfort me. I hate that he had tried to stop me from breaking, for that broke me more. His comfort tortured me. I knew I should leave, but I couldn't. I felt something, a lot for him. He could have left, but he was not brave enough to. Instead, he waited and I suffered still. Till I died over and over again inside.' She would tell you about how we met. The first time she saw me was while she sat on that wooden stool and her head was held between the thighs of someone who weaved her hair while she whistled away, and I walked in with her brother who introduced me as his friend, the one he always talked about. She would tell you of all the things that I said to her that day with my eyes that my mouth could not say. She would tell you about the footprints those things left in her heart as I left her house that day without saying a word to her. She would tell you how those footprints remained there until a month later when she bumped into me in school, in front of the Senate building, under the supervisory gaze of the sun. She would tell you about the first time she was in my room. How she sat on the chair and watched me, sitting on the table, playing a mouth organ that stirred hormones inside of her.

Depending on how close you both are, or how willing she is to open up to you (she opens up pretty easily), She would tell you about how I had bent over and kissed her, on her nose first, then her lips. Softly. And how my tongue slid into her mouth, as if searching for myself inside of it. She would tell you, sniffing and trying vainly to swallow the knob that sits in her throat, about how it seemed like I rescued her from the thickest layers of darkness. About how I seemed like the hand that pulled her out of the emotional mud she was drowning in. About how she had pulled out of it, heaving and gasping, and how she wholeheartedly caste herself upon me, hopelessly. 'For him', She would say, her eyes now glistening with beads of tears that rolls down her cheeks, 'I changed. I made myself perfect. For him. He seemed like a sanctuary. Oh, how I should have known. It felt cold and dark inside, and that should have scared me. But it didn't. Instead, I saw in it a comfortable place to lay. How was I supposed to know that the cold, damp, empty space inside of him was a forbidden place to seek refuge in?' She would tell you about how the fire stopped glowing as it used to, and how she had talked to me about it, and how I had been so full of reassurance. She would tell you about how we talked less and less every time we finished making love, and how at the end we stopped talking altogether.

She would tell you of the awkwardness that seemed to lay between the both of us like a third, mystical person after we were done swimming in the pool of ecstasy. How suddenly it seemed like I was drenched in shame, like I had committed some sort of abomination for touching her at all. She would say how it seemed like suddenly my skin started to shrink in disgust every time she touched me. How when she held my hands I slipped away like fine sand slips through one's fingers. 'One day', she would say, her stare pinned on nothing in particular, not looking at you yet not looking at anything at all, 'I kissed him, and his lips were cold like the surface of some steel left outside on a cold night. Inside, he was stiff, and nothing moved. They were dead! I swear, the butterflies were dead!' She would then lean back, and shake her head, and smile. The sort of smile that accentuates the pains that knocked against one's chest. Then she would continue— 'It was then that I knew he was gone. I just didn't know where, but he was gone.' She would sniff again. 'I should have left immediately I noticed, but I was lost. Lost inside of him. Wherever he wandered to, he took me to and he didn't even know. But I was there. I just didn't know where. I had tried to search inside of him, to see where he was drifting to. To see if I was losing him to another girl. But I could see nothing. Heartbreaks hurt less if they happen once. But for every time I looked into his eyes, I saw less of him, and that broke a tiny part of my heart. Bits by bits, I was tearing apart, and he knew, and he could have left, and save me the slow death, but he didn't. He tried to comfort me with his presence, yet, he tortured me with it.' Everything she would say about me will be true, because somehow, we are all villains in

172

somebody's story. How could she not have known that I was the one who ran to her, even as she thought she ran to me? How could she not have known, that I had clung to her, like one clings to a tree branch when he's falling, because I was too afraid to admit to myself what I really was? How could she not have known that I was with her because I needed to feel like a man?

This is what she would not tell you. She would not tell you that one night she had come to my house without notice, hoping to find the answers to questions that plagued her. Jane, her instincts are out of this world. Sharp. Sensitive, especially when hurt. She would not tell you this, for the sake of the times we live in, especially for those of my kind. She would not tell you that she had stood in front of my door, knocking, laden with the gratitude of validation and the hurt of an impending discovery. She had known, that whatever was happening in the room at that time had to be a ritual of an erotic intimacy. She had known by the way the curtains were drawn fully down over the windows even though it was warm outside. She had known by the caution with which the door was locked; hooked up, down, and keyed at the centre. Locked in a deliberate attempt to conceal something sensitive. She had known because of my hesitation to open the door. She had known, just by looking at me while I stood at the door, my shorts dangling loosely around my waist, and the fire in my eyes. The same fire that had died with her had suddenly been awoken by another girl. But she shoved me aside and looked inside the room, and it was a guy she saw, trying vainly to feign an artificial detachment from the situation by pressing his phone casually. But she knew without even asking, because she is Jane. She said nothing. She just turned and walked away, and as she disappeared into the night it seemed like I saw her pulling her heart wearily behind her like a traveling box.

'You are an abomination!' She screamed at me, inside of her room the next day. Then, in a sudden surge of sobriety, her voice quivering, and she said: 'Was I not good enough? Was it so bad that you had to leave me for a dick?' 'It's not you Jane', I said,

'It's not about you. It's about me. I have felt this way since a long time ago.' 'But, what happened? What changed you?' She asked, brows furrowed in a concerned inquisition, like a mother sincerely worried about something strange she just discovered about her child. 'Nothing. I guess this was how I was made.' 'Made?' She scoffed, 'by who? God? God created everyone perfect!' I had not gone to her to get back to her. I had gone to apologise for putting her through all I did. For opening the door to an empty room for her. For making her reach for something I knew did not exist. For running to her for help even when she needed one herself. So, I left her place, never to return. I left her place, knowing that she thinks that I, along with all of my kind, are not God's perfect creation. Maybe, just maybe she was right. But just maybe, we are God's little mistakes.

The Writer

Victor Daniel is a Nigerian student of Law who likes to travel, read short stories and write some himself. Some of his short stories have been in The Kalahari Reviews and a couple of widely read anthologies. He has two ebooks to his name and he's a Wallflower.

Mobile: +2349050998205

Email: vdslim1@gmail.com

Facebook: vdslim1

174

Would Be Not

by Deborah Tiyan

He stood perched by the girder on the corridor, staring down at the figure in checkered white and peach, seated on the wooden bench under the mango tree. Their school was a big one. Four blocks of three storied buildings, all enclosing the garden. And so, standing by the banister, on the second floor of the senior's block, he watched the ebony black beauty, head bowed, tugging at her neck-length cornrows clearly lost in thoughts.

After much contemplation, he turned back and climbed down the flight of stairs, eagerly moving towards her.

He thought of saying Hi, but instead sat, hoping she'd turn to see who encroached her space. She didn't as much blink, and so he observed her, only just realizing how much he enjoyed watching her. Ever since she walked into his classroom, and ultimately his life, he could never get tired of staring at her. Her features were as familiar to him as the lines on his palm.

She spoke without looking up. "Seeing anything Interesting?"

The venom of the question was lost in the softness of her voice. "Matter of fact, I am."

"What do you want?" She asked weakly. "I came here to hear myself think, and having the cutest boy in class leering over me, isn't helping."

"You think I'm cute?"

"Duh, everyone thinks you're cute."

"Thank you."

"It wasn't a compliment."

He smiled, picking up a fallen leaf. "So why are you out here, hearing thoughts, when you are supposed to be in there –

"pointing to the road leading to the cafeteria, he continued. "– eating lunch."

"I'm not hungry."

Her stomach growled.

"Your tummy doesn't seem to agree with you." He said, stifling laughter.

"Stupid worms," she accused, pressing her palms against the waist band of her skirt. "Fine, I'm avoiding someone."

"David?"

She turned and gazed intently at him. "Stalker much?"

"It's him then." He rubbed his hands together. "It's not a hard nut to crack. The whole school knows you both are an item."

"Were." She corrected, trailing shapes on the sand with the tip of her shoe.

"I'm sorry."

"Yeah."

"Want to talk about it?"

"No."

"Okay."

"Okay."

Her stomach growled again, and this time she laughed. "I think I'll get that lunch now."

"Then we'd better hurry, the bell goes off in five minutes."

"You're coming with me?"

"Of course, after hearing yours' sing, their brethren in my stomach seem to have started a rebellion."

She laughed, and he felt something stir within him. "You should laugh more often, hiding that dentition from the public, should be considered illegal."

176

"Mr. Dimple has got a sweet tongue." She laughed.

"Faith speaking?" He joked.

"If we don't get going now, not even a spoonful of flour crusts would be left." She got up, stretching out her hand to him. He took it.

"I guess this makes us friends now?"

"Friends, we are."

Two months from then, 17-year-old Anthony, would introduce his first love to his Mother, as his girlfriend.

Six months later Gloria sat on the kitchen counter, legs swinging, watching an aproned Anthony stir a steaming pot. He reached for the pepper shaker in the open cupboard above his head and shook profusely into the cooking pot. Gloria sprang to her feet, dashing to snatch the seasoning from him.

"That's too much pepper, idiot," she laughed, peeling the pepper shaker from his hand. "It's yam porridge, not pepper soup."

"The only two dishes you know how to prepare." He mumbled under his breath.

"What did you just say?"

"Nothing baby, you heard something?" his eyes were dancing.

"Better."

"Okay, so…what to add next?" he turned and stared hopefully at her.

"Mr. All knowing, asking for directions?" She arched an eyebrow. "Fine, Groundnut oil."

"Serious?"

"Yeah."

"Then how's it supposed to come out red?" he asked confusedly, stirring the porridge.

"The spices would react with the oil, then the colour would change." she replied, trying to suppress the rupturing laughter forming in her throat.

He stared at her skeptically and turned back to do what he was told.

Lifting the lid few minutes later, he gaped dazedly into the pot. "What happened?"

"What happened where?" She asked innocently.

"Fool me once Gloria, fool me once." He sang, nodding his head slowly.

Unable to control herself anymore, she flung her 5'7 body to the ground, giving into the explosive laughter that engulfed her. Anthony, staring from the pot, to her and then back to the pot, couldn't deny the humour of the scene, burst out laughing too.

"Mum is definitely going to crack once she sees what her to be future daughter-in-law prepared for lunch." He said, using his index finger and thumb to smoothen an imaginary beard.

"You wouldn't dare." She replied, her face contorted in a frozen laughter.

Winking at her, he hobbled out of the kitchen and she sprinted off after him.

Tina slumped onto the green sofa, the only settee in the sitting room which she could comfortably stretch her legs, hissing for the umpteenth time. She thought of all the places she could have been in but instead sat idly at home, drenched in her own sweat as the stupid power company hadn't deemed it fit to provide electricity.

School had resumed two weeks ago, but sure lectures weren't going to commerce until about a week after, she decided to stay back home.

178

But it was the second week and she was meant to leave for school today. Her Dad was supposed to drop her off, but unfortunately an office emergency had come up and he had to attend to that. She had suggested taking public transport but he would have none of it.

She yanked off her ear plugs, stuffing them into the hollow of the chair. She hissed again, picking up the novel she had unsuccessfully been trying to read since the last five hours.

That was when she heard the screaming.

He had gone into the bathroom to take a shower, no thanks to the blazing heat, while she laid on his bed with outstretched legs crossed at the ankle, leafing through an old newspaper.

"Mom wants me to fill in UNN as my first choice for Jamb." She said as soon as he emerged from the bathroom, his white singlet clung to his wet bod, and his jeans, unhooked, hung loosely around his waist.

She squinted up at him, head to foot. "You went in without your towel again. How many times do I have to remind you?"

He bent his head forward, sweeping out water from his hair with his right hand and smiled. "It was intentional this time." He went over to where she lay and pretended to pick up a clothing item, stopped halfway and planted a quick kiss on her cheek. "Not everyone is cold-blooded like you." She picked up a pillow to throw at him and he doubled back, running to the end of the room to avoid being hit.

She laughed as the pillow still met him square on his leg. He picked up the pillow, and drew to sit on the bed's edge closest to her, his back towards her. His face now wore a solemn expression. "So, we won't be schooling together then."

"Not if you apply to the same school."

"That's impossible Gloria, you know Dad –"

"Yeah, I know." She reached to stroke his arm. "Dad is a professor in Unilag, and therefore admission into school is sealed." She completed. "I understand, it's just…" unable to find the right words, she kept mum.

He turned and stared at her. "I miss you."

She smiled. " I'm still here. We haven't even written Jamb yet."

"I know, but I also know how miserable not seeing you for a day makes me feel, much more a month – or two –or three –or four."

Seeing the feigned puppy dog look on his face, she doubled over laughing. Straightening to her knees, she hugged him from behind, her face to the back of his neck. "I miss you too."

He paused, sniffing wildly. "Can you smell that?"

"Smell what?" following suit, she sniffed around.

"Like something burning – shit"

"– Oh my gosh." They interjected at the same time. Both made for the door, running hysterically towards the kitchen.

Oozing from the gaping brown mahogany door, were curlicues of dispersing white smoke. "No, no, no," Anthony kept muttering as he skipped down the stairs, his breath catching in his chest. Gloria got to the landing first, and darted into the kitchen.

Maybe if she wasn't so caught up searching for the mittens, and then too busy lifting the pot with its incinerated content to the sink, she would have noticed he didn't get into the kitchen but merely stood by the door frame.

Maybe if her eyes weren't misty from the stinging effect of the smoke, she would have seen him leaning by the door, clutching at his chest.

Maybe if her ears weren't blocked by her own profuse coughing, she would have heard his urgent wheezing amidst his stifled cough.

Maybe if she weren't so tied up, knotting the window curtain by the kitchen sink to let in fresh air, she might have heard him call out her name.

180

Maybe if she had known he wasn't acting the part, she wouldn't have walked up to him, teary-faced from the smoke, jokingly calling him a cry baby.

Maybe if he had told her he was asthmatic, she never would have let him cook in the first place.

Maybe if he, in a bid to hide his sickness from her, hadn't hidden his albuterol medication in his travelling bag, at the topmost cupboard of his room when he knew she was visiting, she would have known where to find it as soon as the symptoms and his hand gestures made sense to her.

Maybe if she had immediately called his mom, instead of screaming; which drew in Tina, the next-door neighbor to house, she might have directed her to where the spare was kept.

Maybe if Tina had paid attention in Biology class, she wouldn't have attempted a Holly wood version of administering CPR to an asthmatic patient during an attack, instead of an ABC.

But unfortunately, an infinite number of maybes couldn't overturn the advent of a future that would be not – a future with Anthony.

And so, as Anthony's head lay fidgety on her laps, mouthing the incoherent words of one made delusional from lack of oxygen, he lost consciousness.

Which he never regained.

The Writer

Mobile: +2349021980131

Email: debbietiyan02@gmail.com

Instagram: Theo_ziny

Strings of Desperation

by Jeff Ugochukwu Emmanuel

We are in Agadez, Niger Republic. We are traipsing towards a run-down structure. The smell of dust, tobacco, and urine is everywhere. I am flanked by nine other girls; going to Europe, from Nigeria, and we do not know each other. Though we are not acquainted, but we are like a bracelet of finely cut, shiny little spangles; trilling, tingling, and rubbing against each other. A soft music of hope, and promise, swelling with every step. The moonlight is a diffuse ocean above us, expelling the clingy blackness of the night, and giving life and purpose to the times.

The haphazardness of this place pours into me, and reminds me of home— of my baby sister, Ini. We had a family ritual when our parents yet lived. We believe that a cheerful moon has astronomical positive energy and when channeled; it gallops, and can caress the heartstrings of unfeeling men, causing them to daydream about little flitting butterflies of extravagant colors. Today the moon is fulsome and merry. I look up into it and say a quiet prayer. I am sure Ini is tucked away in the embrace of softness, smiling, and dreaming about the myriad possibilities of tomorrow.

The girl beside me dips and backs up. I recede to check her out. The others don't notice. They keep moving, but I mouth something incoherently, bringing their attention back to us. She is holding onto her neck. Legs akimbo. Her face is pale, and sweaty. She is wheezing, and her breath is rapid, and the coughing won't stop. She points to the bag hanging from her shoulder. I reach into it, fumbling for a reliever inhaler. The others are watching, rattled, unsure of what to do or say. Some of them say sorry, but it does not come out. They are soaked with too much compassion to rouse any words of definite sharp edges. She takes one puff of the inhaler every thirty seconds, up to a maximum of ten puffs. The symptoms begin to fizzle out. She says the elephant sitting on her chest is gone.

We proceed, this time languidly. She is leaning against me for support. I let her wear my bandanna over her nose to filter the poisoned air. Between the girls, I can feel a million questions strewing, and loitering, for when time allows. I have a few of mine. We go past two sentries, past an open jeep, past two other sentries in front of the building; and at each point, they exchange words with our escort— words we do not understand. They are minors, these sentries, and their youthful eyes won't leave our breasts.

It is dim inside and the air is more pristine. A sliver of moonlight spills into the room, through the slanted louvers, Illuminating the vacuum some more. Our escort trips into a distant pathway. The room is silent. There is uncertainty lingering. We are sitting, our bods snuggling like phrases that cannot make perfect meaning on their own. She looks at me, the asthmatic patient; head askew, and says my name is Omah. My name is Julie, I say. Thank you for helping me, she says again, radiating gratitude. The other girls begin to introduce themselves, and soon we are seams of longing, abutting, finding perfection in the tiny strings of desperation that binds and makes us whole.

I ask Omah why she is here in her condition. The girls are dying to ask the same question. Omah says she has two little brothers, alone in the world. Even though she couldn't go to school herself, she is determined to send them to school. Good schools. Nothing has worked for her in Nigeria, even prostitution is fraught with stiff competition. Her voice starts to break. I throw my arm around her, gently. We are bonding. All of us are eager to tell our tale. The next girl, Tonia; awkward and graceless. She says her mom sent her here. Her mom says she is tired of providing for two people. The Nigerian men at the brothels do

184

not fancy her. She is no good to anyone; maybe the men in Europe will find good use for her. The next girl, Ese; firm and resolute, with a face that lights up the whole of Niger. She says she does not know her mother; just the treasured memories of her short life, passed on by her late father. He died when she was fifteen. Her uncles confiscated his properties. She joined the streets, and they have shown her no clemency. But if Europe is kind, she would come back, and visit her uncles with a wrath that is sure and swift.

Our escort comes back out, disrupting the moment. Her finger curls to Ije, and she follows her back through the same course. Ije does not come back. Ese and others follow subsequently, and none of them comes back out. I am next. I trail this escort, hot on her heels. We make a right, past a guard, into another hallway with identical doors on each side. We keep moving, until we come to the last door, to the left. It is a connection to the other side. A cluster of buildings, walls smudged with sleazy graffiti, multiple doors from every side, and it leaves you wondering where they lead. I am queasy and ill, and everywhere funks of musk and infamy.

This escort points me to a door leading into a room and scrambles away. A man, queer and curt, with a voice that fills space is sitting across the room. Above him are atomic lights, whirling, and spraying happy colors across the surface. My eyes comb for the girls, but I don't see any of them. He shows me to a seat in front of him. Circling around me lazily; he cuts strands of my hair, finger nails, three cuts at the back of the neck; each ingredient into a receptacle, and every movement promises a different incantation. I am receptive until he asks me to remove my panties. I ask what all of these have to do with my panties. He says it is for an oath taking. That is how they ensure the girls come back to repay their sponsors, and if they don't, they die painfully. The door is always open if you do not want any of this.

185

He carries the halo of someone who is doing me a huge favor. Not exertive or persuasive. Nothing. I remove my panties. He cuts hair from my pubic parts. Reciting gibberish after him, I gulp down the content of this receptacle. And by God, a cosmic part of my soul inhabits it.

He calls for the guard at the door. Take her, he says, and turns to me; eyes half lidded, mouth twisting: do as you are told from here on out, everything depends on it. We walk out of the room, each foot placed carefully where the other vacates. We go past a dark alley, into an enclosure, and down to a cellar. This place, in the cellar, is a rectangle of lurid red, and music is thumping from everywhere. I am static, absorbing a world I do not fit into. A pitch-colored man is dancing on the stage. He is lusty and unclad to his cock. A harem of honey-colored women are moving convincingly to his tune. The girls on the rostrum are bare and slinky; green eyebrows extending to their temples, heels high, liquor rolling on their skin, and they nestle and lap from each other. One guy is cartwheeling. A girl abets him; her mouth bouncing gently on his cock like hydraulics. They take the form of a catapult. Everyone here is springy: they are a rubic cube puzzle of different shades: shifting with abandon, and converging to remain singular.

A guy comes to collect me. The blackest and shortest man I have ever seen. He brings me to a doorway; his head moves in a silent command. There are three men inside. They are set. They are gaping at me, but they do not talk. They spring all over me like a swarm of bees. I try to wriggle away but their hold is steady. I don't stop trying still. Bawling. Whinging. Kicking. Finally, one says with a deep voice, and an accent that is thick and elastic: you best keep still, if you wish to travel with the others tomorrow. His words conspire to kill what little fight is left in my broken spirit. I have persevered and journeyed this far, and If this is what it takes to ensure my sister gets the good life, then amen.

Morning

186

Piping chortles heave— rising and falling—ruckus sprouting to fill in the gaps; a bright coppery sun is skimming the horizon, as new morning bedlam rises. We are sitting in an open jeep. Our minds chewing on the events of yesterday, but our tongues are unable to string together any words of coherent drift, so we let our eyes fall on each other— regarding and gleaning; hoping that by some miracle, we find peace in the choices we have made. We are heading to Tripoli, the Libyan capital, through the Sahara, and I can't help but worry for Omah.

The coast of Tripoli: a morass of people traffic and a mishmash of jostling struggles. Voices are tussling to topple themselves, pitches littered, and the brisk and warm Mediterranean Sea air is circling and circling and it breathes inside your head like a coconut, unfaltering and drenches out everything significant, even the tiniest little thoughts. We meet our sponsor for the first time. A thick-set, ebony woman. We are gathered in one place, waiting for the boat that sails to Italy. It arrives, the boat—a dinghy. Hundreds of people are scrambling to get in. The girls too. People open their legs for another to seat in between. Packed. They sail. Another comes around. Same thing happens again. The last one comes around. The girls are shouting at me to get in. I freeze. Time is whizzing past and you pray it slows down. Time is you getting a pedicure, and it leaves a slight perforation at the edge of your biggest toe. The spindly toe next, niggles at it because there is pleasure that makes the pain sweet. Sweet pain. Spindly niggles and niggles until the sweetness silently drifts away. Pain is all there is, and it spreads. And you struggle to get spindly to stop because the movement is almost involuntary.

Before me is unbounded panorama corrugating, whirling, and straggling as far as the eyes can see. Same blush adjoining to form a curve that falls far behind me—a world that is blue, misty and unclear. All we have to test this vast world is an overload dinghy. The odds are staked firmly against us. I am unable to see any flickers in all of the chaos. I had promised my sister a better life, not a bloated body, half-naked, face discolored and hands with skin peeling off in large chunks, floating face-down near the water's edge. The world is darn cold, and I cannot leave her alone in it. Not while it is in my power. Omah, in a bid to convince me says, sometimes you have to shut your eyes and just make a leap, and hope that when you land, you don't break a leg. If I know anything about life, it is this: that when the stakes are higher, we do not pleasure in taking risks, and if ever we do, it is because what is on the other side is worth the candle. However, when events begin to wind down; we like to kid ourselves that we are there because we had dared to hope. Hope is just a puff in the air, believe is the wind that gives it power and direction. Standing here, it is much easier for me to just try to hope, but deep inside I do not have the believe to make this final leap. I bid the girls farewell, and ramble into the city of Tripoli, and from there I will find my way back to Nigeria. And back to my sister.

Much later, I stray into an establishment. It is owned by an Algerian. Here, I learn that none of the boats that left this morning made it into Europe. They all sank in the Mediterranean Sea. It is all over the news. They say there are few survivors rescued by the Italian authorities. The rank and file are distempered and the people stink. They blame the European Governments. They blame war. They blame everything; even the sea. The countries have all their defenses up. My feet slip into my belly. The air around me pauses for a moment. Time is suspended and images become blurry. I manage to muster and mumble a few words of supplication: that If perhaps the girls didn't make it, and if there is ever a God and some golden paradise bundled up somewhere, I hope they get recompense. I pray they get a look-in. Nigeria was hell enough.

The Writer

188

Jeff Ugochukwu Emmanuel is a Nigerian writer and editor who works at Creative Freelance Writers Nigeria. He is an acute observer of people and geography. When he is not writing, he is traveling to places in the pages of a book.

Mobile: +2348064952739

Email: jeffomenyuru@gmail.com

Facebook: jeff.u.emmanuel

About the Authors

These stories are not the products of writers who have been decorated or recommended for ground breaking epiphanies. This is simply storytelling, it's about heart and passion. Jonathan Oladeji and his team at cfwriterz.com believe they can give voice to stories that you may have not encountered from Africa. They have gathered some grassroot storytellers. Young Nigerians, Africans who have no need to paint Africa from any other lens than the one their nation has handed to them. This is family, this is home. They are not worried that these stories would not receive your standing ovations, they are worried that you would look at the nakedness of their hearts and marvel at their strength and resolve. These stories just had to be told.

About the Book

This collection contains stories from 30 young Africans. The idea to publish an anthology which was also a collaborative book came up while the cfwriterz community began to gain momentum and grow. The admin and moderators had been seeking opportunity to create a larger audience and reach for members. Monica Kunzekweguta became the channel for this dream to come to fruition. This collaborative effort between cfwriterz.com (registered as CF Media and Brand PR Services) and Authors Without Boundaries is one of the community's efforts to dismantle all the red tape attached to the growth and recognition of stories from Africa.